CLEVELAND CLASH
3

Keeping SCORE

ELLEY ARDEN

CRIMSON
ROMANCE
F+W Media, Inc.

Published by
Crimson Romance
an imprint of F+W Media, Inc.
10151 Carver Road, Suite 200
Blue Ash, OH 45242. U.S.A.
www.crimsonromance.com
ISBN 10: 1-4405-8952-6
ISBN 13: 978-1-4405-8952-2
eISBN 10: 1-4405-8953-4
eISBN 13: 978-1-4405-8953-9

To Adam and Leanna,
may you live happily ever after

Chapter One

"Where the hell is Glenn?"

Rome Rizzelli stormed into the office of WKST's new station owner and gave her his best Liam Neeson–style "Did you kidnap my daughter?" look.

"I fired him," Amelia said, wearing that same smug look her old man had given Rome six months ago when he'd yanked *Riled Up with Rome* from drive time on Sports Radio 94.7 and moved it to the dead zone of midmorning.

"That's what Glenn said."

"Well, then, if Glenn already told you I fired him, why are you glowering in my office on a Saturday morning?"

"Because I want you to hire him back. He's been my producer for ten years!"

"Ten years too long." She crossed her arms and lifted her chin. "I'm older than you, Rome, remember? I've been in and out of this station for twenty years. I remember the day my father hired you straight out of OSU. O-H!" she said as a reminder they shared an alma mater, and then she sat there good and quiet until Rome gave in and added an unenthusiastic, "I-O."

She smiled briefly. "The show is stale, Rome."

"I disagree. It's the time slot."

"I don't think so. Your numbers were down before you moved to ten."

"I'm sure my numbers were better than that syndicated crap your father put in my place."

She dismissed him with a shrug. "Only barely and your show costs more."

He winced. Rome knew this business was all about ratings, but how could Glenn's ten years of faithful service to this station be tossed aside so easily?

He shoved his hands into his longer-than-normal hair and tugged at the roots. "Glenn has a kid headed to college this fall. How the hell is he going to pay tuition without a job?"

"Not my problem." Amelia tapped her fingers on a folder stuffed with paper. "This is my problem, pages and pages of numbers so bad I can't fathom why my father didn't sell this place before he died. The day Barry Vincent left to start his own station, the war was on. And we never really recovered financially. So, like it or not, I had to do what I had to do. And trust me; you wouldn't have liked the alternative."

The minute she'd mentioned Barry's name, Rome's nose wrinkled. He'd trusted that guy, like an older brother, to teach him the ropes, and the biggest lesson he'd ended up learning was you couldn't trust anyone in radio—except Glenn. "What was the alternative to keeping Glenn?"

"Firing you."

Shit.

"Which still might happen, because I can't justify paying you the top salary at this station when your show is four hours of mostly berating callers and taking the unpopular stance on everything."

"I'm a shock jock, Amelia." He threw up his hands. "That's what I do. Listeners like it."

She slapped her hand on the folder. "Advertisers don't. You lost O'Reilly's Family Restaurants because of that prank call you and Glenn made yesterday."

Oh, come on! That call had been hilarious. He still couldn't believe Glenn had gotten him through to Cleveland Boltz general manager Patrick Swift.

Rome stifled a laugh. "Hey, Swift is the one who got himself into this mess by paying for sex in the first place, and he hung up on us thirty seconds into the call. What's the big deal?"

"The big deal is a chain of *family* restaurants that was paying us more than $15,000 a year in ad dollars doesn't want to be associated with a radio show whose host is prank calling around town pretending to be a violent pimp collecting on bad debts."

"Listeners loved it! The phones were ringing off the hook."

"Yes, but again, the people at O'Reilly's hated it, and I did, too."

"So that's why Glenn was fired?"

She nodded. "And if you want to avoid his fate, you're going to start doing things differently."

"How differently?"

She sat back in her oversized leather chair and smiled. "Say hello to your new producer."

Even as his stomach bottomed out, he looked over her shoulder and into the hall hoping to see someone else, but nobody was there. It was just Rome and ... "No!" He glared at her. "Please tell me you're joking."

Her smile broadened. "Nope. I'm producing. At least temporarily, until I can find someone else I think you'll listen to."

Shit.

"I have big plans for you, Rizzelli. Starting tonight."

He gave her a puzzled look. "I'm off tonight."

"Not anymore. I arranged a remote broadcast from Ballers', that bar across the street from John Heisman Stadium."

"Why the hell would we want to go all the way out there?"

"The Cleveland Clash have a playoff game."

Wait. That was *women's* pro football. This station had never covered a single women's event—not even during an Olympic year. "You've got to be kidding me."

"Nope. When I asked the folks at O'Reilly's restaurants what we could do to win back their business, they said be more inclusive and listener-friendly."

"You've got to be kidding me," he said again.

As the older brother of a woman with Down syndrome, he was all for inclusivity, but ... this was sports radio they were talking about. The audience he'd been pandering to for the last ten years wasn't made up of the kind of guys who wanted to hear about women's football.

"We're going to lose some longtime listeners," he said.

"Then we'll gain new ones."

"It's not that easy."

"It is." She narrowed her eyes. "And you don't have a choice here. You're doing this show tonight."

Amelia was wrong, but it didn't matter. He was going to end up paying for the drop in ratings no matter how he looked at it.

Rome clenched his jaw and shook his head before saying, "Fine." But she wasn't going to like what he had to say. Bottom line ... if he was going to be fired no matter what he did, he was going to go out in a blaze befitting ten years of stirring up trouble on the airwaves.

He stalked out of her office and into the hall only to have his ringing cell phone slow his pace. His sister's name and gummy-grinned face flashed on the screen, and instantly, his mood changed.

Rome blew out the anger he'd been holding in and smiled. "Hey, kiddo. What's up?"

"The ceiling, the sun, the sky."

He chuckled even though it was the same exchange they had every time she called. "You're a goof."

"Just like you."

They definitely shared an off-the-wall sense of humor. "What's going on?"

"Will you bring me home a milkshake?" Her voice was muffled like maybe she was covering her mouth and the receiver with her hand to avoid their mother getting wind of this.

"You're lactose intolerant, Tess."

"Not today."

He bit back a laugh. "I'm sorry to tell you, but you're lactose intolerant every day."

"I know." She sounded sad and even farther away.

"Where are you making this call?"

"In my closet."

So that their mother, who was on permanent disability due to a fall from an electrical company ladder truck fourteen years ago, didn't hear. Despite her limited mobility and all the other medical issues she'd endured from the accident, there was nothing wrong with her ears ... or her mouth.

"How 'bout I bring you all home some donuts?"

"Glazed," Tess said, and he could hear her smiling.

"You bet. Ask Mom what she wants, too."

He made his way to his car while he waited for Tess to gather their order. In the background, he could hear his mother complaining.

"I don't want donuts. I don't feel good. I'm in too much pain. I need my pills."

"Tell her I'll be home soon and not to bother Aunt Karen."

For the millionth time since Rome had hired his aunt to help care for his mother and sister, he thought he didn't pay her nearly enough. Karen came for a few hours a day, five days a week. But he wouldn't be able to keep paying her or anyone else a damn thing if he lost his job.

As much as he wanted to stick it to Amelia for firing Glenn, maybe he should at least *try* to play it her way tonight. But then he thought about the conversation Glenn must be having with his family right now, and giving in to Amelia felt like selling out on a guy who'd been with Rome through thick and thin. *No way.* He wasn't turning his back on what he and Glenn had built. He would go to Ballers'. He would even talk about women's football. But he was going to do it his way and prove to Amelia the audience was on his side.

After all, there was safety in numbers.

•••

Sixty-four sweaty, screaming women piled into the home team locker room at John Heisman Stadium on the far west side of Cleveland, Ohio.

"Oh-and-four is ancient history!" Jade Wren launched herself onto the back of her roommate, Jillian Bell, joyful that the Cleveland Clash had shed their rough start and made it into the playoffs. "Round Two here we come."

Jillian reached back with one tattoo-riddled arm and roughed up Jade's hair. "We need tunes ... and drinks. I got our usual tables reserved at Ballers', and I'm buying shots for everybody!"

Tanya Martin, who anchored the Clash O-line with Jade, gave Jillian some side-eye. "Easy tiger. We get one day off, and then it's back on the field again Monday. We gotta face New York next week."

"New York has to face *us*," quarterback MJ Rooney said with a confident smile.

Jade let go of Jillian and soaked up the sounds of victory. She loved these women. For an overprotected only child, they were the perfect surrogate family.

"Please tell me you can skip going out for ice cream with your mom and gram tonight," Jillian said hopefully.

Ice cream after every game was the price Jade paid for playing a potentially dangerous sport. Not that ice cream itself was a hardship. But luckily, tonight was a rarity. "Actually, they couldn't make the game. Umma wasn't feeling well. But I'm still going to have to call and check in. She's going to want to grill me about any hits I took, and Halmoni will want to add any new bruises to her running tally. But I'll make it quick. Promise."

Tanya reached her locker first, tossing her helmet onto the top shelf with a triumphant clang. "It's a miracle they support you playing at all."

MJ reached out and pulled Jade into a playful headlock. "Of course they do. Best center in the FFL right here, ladies!"

More hoots and hollers.

Jade reveled in the noise even as her thoughts turned darker. The real reason her otherwise very traditional mother and grandmother supported her football career was because this game made her tough. After what the three of them had been through at the hands of her alcoholic, abusive father, having a daughter who was strong enough to protect herself outweighed any other concerns they may have had.

She pulled off her shoulder pads and shoved the sobering thoughts aside. "Jill, I thought you said we needed some music?"

And that was all it took. A half undressed Jillian grabbed her phone and walked the line of benches like a balance beam on her way to the portable speaker they'd used to pregame.

"Put on something we know," Tanya teased. "None of that alt crap you peddle to the clubs."

Jillian was a band promoter for her day gig, and her roster was mostly punk, ska, metal hybrids. She stuck out her tongue to a locker room full of laughter and slapped her phone onto the speaker's dock. "I'm like Santa Clause, and you get what I give, Martin. In fact, I'm just going to push play and see what comes up."

"What were you listening to last?" Jade asked, because that was exactly what would come up.

A rich, rough male voice emanated from the speaker, filling the locker room, startling more than a few of them. Probably because he wasn't singing. He wasn't even rapping. He was simply talking ... about them.

I'm coming to you live tonight, folks, and get this: my new producer told me our topic this evening is the Cleveland Clash.

All of a sudden, you could've heard a feather drop in that room. Then Jillian opened her mouth and said, "I had on Sports Radio 94.7. That's Rome Rizzelli! He's talking about us …"

"Ssh!" Tanya jumped up on the bench and waved her hands above her head. "I want to hear what he has to say."

This was crazy. In all the months Jade had been listening to 94.7, she'd never once heard a host talk about women's sports, especially not that outrageous jerk, Rome Rizzelli.

MJ's hand landed on Jade's shoulder. "If he says something nice about us, I'll take back every bad thing I've ever said about him. Well, most of the bad things."

For some reason, Jade's stomach was jumpy. What were the odds a guy who trashed almost everyone would say something positive about them?

The background noise from the bar crackled through the speakers and another male voice could be heard yelling, "Who the hell are they?" And still another hollered, "Who cares?"

Rome laughed.

"Once an asshole …" MJ said.

They are Cleveland's full tackle women's football team, and apparently, they played a first-round playoff game tonight and won, so my producer cares. Personally, I don't, because there are enough A-list sports in this great city to cover without dipping into the B list. I don't cover soccer, either. He made a disgusted noise. Besides, I honestly don't think you care, and I'm nothing without my listeners. I need listeners to keep my job, and man, I really want to keep my job. So, correct me if I'm wrong. Do you care about women's football?

Some negative noises echoed in the background, and then Rome made a satisfied sound.

That's what I thought. So there. I talked about the Cleveland Clash. Now, we can move on to more important things.

Jade scrunched up her nose and jumped onto the bench beside Tanya. "Hey! It doesn't matter what that guy and his band of merry idiots think. All that matters is that we care and believe in ourselves. Here's what I think of Rome Rizzelli." She flipped "the bird" at Jillian's phone.

The locker room reenergized.

"It's cool that his producer cares," one of the other linewomen said. The coverage for FFL games was pretty much nonexistent. They barely even got a mention in free community newspapers, never mind prime-time exposure on a hub network like 94.7, which broadcasted to the greater Cleveland metro area.

Still, *any* publicity was not quite the same as good publicity.

"Yeah, that means somebody at that station has a shred of decency, and maybe that person has enough power to eventually fire him!" Jade pumped a fist into the air amid even louder cheers. "Now, shut him off," she said to Jillian. "Let's get ready to party!"

That jerk was not going to ruin their evening.

Chapter Two

Thirty minutes later, sixty-four primped and polished women piled into the bar across the street from John Heisman Stadium. It must've been a sight to see.

Jade wouldn't know, because two steps across the threshold, her phone rang. It was her mother, and she had to take it. She always took it. But never, ever in a bar.

She glanced over her shoulder at the exit, which was blocked by easily more than a thousand pounds of women pushing in, and decided taking a quick left and heading down the narrow staircase to the ladies' room was her best bet.

"I'll catch up with you," she said to Jillian, and then she rushed the stairs with the phone to her ear. "How are you feeling, Umma? I was worried when you didn't answer when I called."

"Where are you? Are you running?"

"No." Jade slowed her pace. "I'm just taking the stairs."

"Good. You're safe at home. That makes me happy. How was the game?"

Jade bit her lip, pushed into the quiet restroom, and did nothing to correct her mother's assumption. Since she'd moved out six months ago and in with Jillian, this was the double life she led. She wasn't exactly proud of the deceit, but she couldn't think of another, better way. How could she possibly explain she'd found fun in the things her mother and grandmother thought as the biggest risks? She didn't want them to worry about her.

"We won."

"Good. Are you hurt?"

"No."

"Did you get hit?"

"Nothing major."

"How many bruises?" But it wasn't her mother's voice; it was her grandmother piping up to be heard.

Jade balanced her phone between her ear and shoulder and lifted her blousy sleeves one at a time. All clear. Then she dragged the soft fabric higher, exposing her belly, and angled her body so she could see the angry, purple welt on her hip. Technically, the trainer had called it a contusion. She touched it briefly and winced. "Tell her no bruises." Then she rolled right into a different subject. "You sound like you're feeling better."

"I am. I had tea, and Mrs. Lee stopped by. That's where I was when you called. In the shop ... meeting her grandson. And guess what?" Jade didn't have to guess. "He wants to meet you." Of course he did. "How about tonight? It's still early. I could send him your way."

"I don't really want to meet him tonight, Umma."

"Why do you want to make me feel bad again? *Be a good girl,* and meet him."

Jade swallowed the discomfort that rose up at that familiar phrase. "Not meeting him doesn't make me a bad person."

"He's from Seoul. Very handsome," her mother added. "He flies a jet."

Okay, that was kind of cool. "Maybe I can work something out tomorrow."

"He'll be gone. He wants to see as much of America as possible while he's here. And trust me, along the way somebody will snatch him up. Did I mention he's tall?"

Jade doubted it. Her mother was just trying to bait her. "How tall?"

"I didn't ask."

Jade straightened from her usual slump to her full five feet, ten inches and eyed herself in the mirror. He was probably five eight at best. Imagine if she wore heels to meet a guy like that?

Not that she was going to give in to the pressure and meet him.

A fast-moving crowd of rowdy women stormed the restroom and pushed her into the corner between the garbage can and towel dispenser. Over the chaos, she heard her mother ask, "What was that noise?"

"Just some people."

"I thought you were home."

Not exactly. "I'm with the team. We wanted to hang out after the win."

The women continued to hog up space in the small room with their bodies and shrill voices.

In the split second of silence between the noise and whatever Jade's mother had been planning to say, one of the women yelled, "I need another drink!"

Umma gasped. "Are you at a bar?"

Busted. Jade bounced her head off the metal towel dispenser. "Yes, but I'm not drinking."

"You know the kind of men who hang out in bars?"

"Your father hung out in bars," Halmoni added, sounding just as clear as if she'd been talking into the receiver.

"You met your loser ex in a bar."

Kyle. Yep. He'd been shooting pool in an off-campus bar, wearing ripped jeans and a killer smile. He could've easily been a fellow Dayton student ... except he'd been thirty, with a rap sheet.

"Don't trust your judgment," her mother said.

"Don't trust men," her grandmother said.

Except Korean men who were handpicked by them.

Jade's free hand fisted at her side. "I'll be fine. You don't have to worry. I'm with the team. I'll call you in the morning."

She ended the call and took a nostril-flaring breath. Good intentions or not, they sure knew how to ruin an evening. And she let them. She let them every time.

Anger squared her shoulders and lifted her chest. Not this time. Not tonight. The sky wasn't going to fall after just one beer. And to prove it, she was heading straight for the bar.

Jade left the restroom on determined strides, the blood whooshing in her ears. And even though the stairs to the bar were narrow and someone was heading down, she charged up anyway. *You're just going to have to move, buddy.*

Glancing up—way up the steep incline—she saw the guy, all blue jeans and James Dean swagger, slow his pace. She slowed hers too as they met in the middle with two free steps in between.

There was a hint of a smile on his face. A little sexy. A little cocky.

This was exactly the kind of man who hung out in bars, exactly the kind of man she shouldn't trust. Broad shoulders, rugged face, and a look in his eyes that said, "Hold on, baby. You're going to enjoy the ride."

Trusting a guy like that was the last thing on her mind.

She smiled, too, until her mother's words of warning echoed in her head. *Don't trust your judgment.*

But they were wrong. She *could* trust her judgment. She'd been on her own for six months now, and nothing terrible had happened. Just because she strayed from the straight and narrow every once in a while didn't mean she was doomed. And to prove it ...

She raised up on her toes, closed the distance between them, and laid one on him. The kiss was sharp and short, like a bold period at the end of a hard-hitting sentence. But before she could pull away, she took a breath, filling her nose with the soft scents of denim, soap, and beer. Her mouth watered. Her brain told her to be still. *Just a little bit longer.*

When, *bam*! He came alive, brushing his lips back and forth across hers in a simple but sensual motion. He skimmed his hand up her hip, raising chill bumps on her skin. And then, he sucked her upper lip between his before he pulled back and whispered, "Hello, there" in a low, dreamy voice that somehow seemed familiar.

"Hi," she whispered back, only to be drowned out by the group of women from the restroom.

They barreled up the stairs behind her amid laughter and a ruckus that made her think about her friends, who were waiting upstairs. *Holy crap!* Talk about getting sidetracked.

The sexy stranger didn't say another word. He just stepped aside to let her pass, but not before he unleashed a killer smile that seemed to be saying, "Come find me later."

But she wouldn't. It was hard to get into any real and lasting emotional trouble when you didn't take your interactions with the opposite sex seriously. That's why she didn't do relationships. Too risky. Her analytical mind preferred calculated risks. Like kissing some guy you would probably never see again—no numbers exchanged, no names.

As the women pushed at her back, she stepped up and up again, and for a split second, Jade and the mystery man finally stood on the same step. He was short! What a shame! A little bit of his sexy shine wore off, which was probably a good thing. All the more reason not to take it beyond one random kiss.

Caught up in the wave of women, Jade climbed the rest of the stairs, still feeling the rush of kissing a perfect stranger in the stairwell. Her mother and grandmother would call that bad judgment. Definitely.

But at the top of the steps, she looked up at the suspended ceiling and smiled. The sky hadn't fallen. She'd kissed a sexy—albeit short—stranger, and absolutely, positively nothing bad had come of it.

Take that, bad judgment.

"Where the hell have you been?" Jillian ran toward her. "And why aren't you answering your texts? You're never going to believe who is here tonight!"

"Who?"

"Rome Freaking Rizzelli! And rumor has it, he's hot! I don't know, though. We haven't seen him yet. He's on a break."

Jade's steps faltered. *A bathroom break?* She swallowed hard. *No. It couldn't be.* But there had been something familiar about that voice.

"Come on!" Jillian pulled on her arm. "You're not going to want to miss this."

Then why did she feel like she absolutely, positively did?

"Okay! Okay!" Jade scrambled along behind her until she stumbled out of the crowd and into an open space.

A long table sat in front of the picture window that overlooked the stadium, from which a huge banner hung, proclaiming The Truth in Sports Talk Radio ... Riled Up with Rome on 94.7. But there was no sign of him.

Tanya Martin rushed up. "His producer just came over to the table. She said she's glad we're here, and she wants us to be rowdy. This is going to be fun!"

Jillian and Tanya high-fived.

Jade felt faint. No. Please tell her she hadn't kissed Rome Rizzelli. It couldn't be. What were the odds? She had a degree in mathematics. She knew all about statistics and probability. This bar was packed. Too packed for her to have stepped on the needle in a haystack.

She stood a little straighter and scanned the crowd for the sexy stranger from the stairs. He had to be here somewhere, swilling draughts with his friends.

"There he is!" Jillian said.

Jade's modern-day James Dean approached the broadcast table, complete with swagger in his step.

Oh dear God, she whispered under her breath. She'd kissed the enemy. She'd *enjoyed* kissing the enemy.

Jillian got in her face. "Can you believe he's *hot?*"

In the bright light of the bar, he was blazing. Shaggy, sandy brown hair covered his head and curled at his temples. His gravelly voice matched the stubbly skin along his chiseled jawline and around what she now knew was a very kissable mouth. But he was a certifiable jerk, who—she watched him raise a pilsner glass of beer to his lips—drank on the job!

She could hear Umma now. *Just like your father, a typical American man.*

"Welcome back, folks. I'm Rome Rizzelli, coming to you live from Ballers' Bar and Grill, where the beer is cold, the wings are hot, and the women are ..." Jade's head spun when he looked straight at her and smiled. "The women are even hotter. Come on down and join me if you've got some time on your hands ..."

Those two little, horrible words roared through her head: *Bad. Judgment.*

There had to be some way to undo what she'd done in that stairwell.

Was it too late to meet Mrs. Lee's grandson?

• • •

Rome looked at his laptop, which displayed basic information about the callers who were on hold, waiting for their chance to speak. The first name was Lewis from Chagrin Falls. Lewis was a regular caller, and the guy liked to stir whatever pot Rome put in front of him. Perfect timing. He needed more proof to show Amelia she'd made a mistake in firing Glenn, and she was barking up the wrong tree by pushing women's sports on an all-male listenership.

"Lewis, how are you, buddy! You're live on the air with Rome. What's going on?"

"Nothing much, man. I'm just hanging out with you. I got a question."

This ought to be good. "Shoot."

"If you had to choose, like if someone was holding a gun to your head, and you had to choose between watching women's football, European soccer, and having a root canal, which would you choose?"

Rome laughed. "Man, that's a tough one."

A ruckus from the corner of the bar drowned out whatever Lewis had said. Rome held the right side of his headphones tighter to his ear and motioned for Amelia to turn up the volume. In the process, he glanced at her, and she was smiling. The hair on the back of his neck stood. *What the hell?*

"I'd probably take the root canal," he said, going for the most outrageous answer, just like his former mentor, that son-of-a-bitch, Barry Vincent had taught him. Though it wasn't so much about following Barry's direction anymore. Now, it was habit.

More noise from the crowd. Boos. That didn't make sense.

He glanced in the direction of the noise. Women—a whole bunch of them—packed around four long tables and lining the wall. Two big ones down in front sneered at him. Where did they all come from? He hadn't noticed them before. In fact, those tables had been empty. He shook his head and refocused on the computer screen, determined not to be rattled.

"Well, now this should be interesting," Amelia's voice practically purred in his headphones. "Let's see how you do with a balanced audience, hotshot."

Unbelievable. Had she set this up? He wouldn't put it past her. Well, he wasn't leaving here until the cheers outweighed the boos again or Amelia kicked him off the air.

"Look, the truth about women's sports is nobody wants to be forced into something. I don't watch women's sports because I don't enjoy women's sports. Most men don't. But we're being forced to pay attention thanks in part to Title XI." The jeers were on overdrive, but the cheers picked up, too. "Seriously. Every time you yell at the television and complain that rules to protect the quarterbacks have watered down the game, thank Title XI. Same thing with new, overreaching concussion protocols. Title XI, thank you for desecrating the games that descended from the greatest warriors on earth: gladiators, charioteers, knights. These men were willing to die for the game. Without true risk, where's the glory?" More boos.

He covered up a surge of panic with a shrug and ended with the ridiculous catchphrase he'd been using for ten years. "That's the truth. You don't like it, you can *Rome* your ass outta here."

It did the trick with his faithful listeners every time. Chants of Rome, Rome, Rome, overtook the boos and put a hearty smile on his face.

No matter how outlandish the stance, he would never be alone out on that ledge. He'd learned that ten years ago when Barry had been the station's demigod. He'd convinced Rome to take a colorful, controversial stance on performance-enhancing drug use in baseball.

"I could use someone else in my corner on this," Barry had said, and Rome being kind of star struck had listened. Some of Rome's on-air antics that day had earned the station a visit from the FCC, particularly his use of the annoying Emergency Broadcasting System's warning tone, which unbeknownst to him had been illegal. And it wasn't until a hefty fine had been levied and Rome had been hauled into the owner's office that he'd learned the whole story. Barry had been playing a prank on him, since at the time, Rome was the lowest ranking on-air personality. It had been station tradition. Fraternity hazing. Only, Rome—in an attempt to be one of the guys—had taken it too far.

The funny thing was, despite all the reprimands, that broadcast had put him on the map, and it had taught him that bold actions and opinions mattered more in this business than reasonable ones.

Tonight would be no different. He punctuated the crowd support with his trademark blast of an air horn, obnoxious but something that wouldn't bring the FCC down on him again.

"I should've fired you this morning, Rome," Amelia said into his headset.

Even though the thought made his stomach roll, if that was where this was headed, at least he was being true to Glenn.

"On to the next caller." He double tapped the mouse pad. "John, you're on the air with Rome."

"I'm totally in support of women's football."

Rome looked up as the cheers became deafening. This go-round, he noticed one of the heftier women was wearing a Cleveland Clash T-shirt. Damn. Not only had Amelia leveled the playing field, she'd leveled it with women football players. That was actually impressive.

But it couldn't last. These women would go home. They wouldn't listen to him every day and call in to the show. Eventually, Amelia would see firsthand that she had a hell of a lot more to lose than to gain by courting some phantom female sports fan demographic.

"Listen, John, it's not that I don't support women playing sports. It's a free country. Play whatever you want to play, but don't expect me to watch it with genuine enthusiasm. I'm never going to watch women's football with the same interest and appreciation as I watch men's football. They're weaker, slower, and smaller. That's not sexist. That's the truth."

"But what if they're wearing lingerie?" John asked suggestively.

Amelia's appalled gasp made Rome smile. This was perfect. He knew his target audience. He played to his target audience. And his target audience was through the roof right now, drowning out the irate noises of Amelia's special guests.

"They have a lingerie football team up in Michigan," John continued. "I've seen a couple games. Everything's hanging out.

Now, that's a women's sport I can get behind. You know what I mean?"

The reasonable, off-air voice in the back of Rome's head groaned. John had gone raunchy. Rome wanted to dial it back a bit. But the part of him that had been performing for ten years coaxed, *Go for broke, buddy.* In this business, shock value equaled name recognition. And if he was going to be out there looking for another job, he was going to need all the name recognition he could get.

Rome took a quick breath and barreled through despite the bad taste in his mouth. "I know what you mean, John. I'd like to get my hands under one of those centers, too."

"We're going to break," Amelia said. "Now."

John's name disappeared from the caller list and music filled Rome's headset. The women at the tables were glaring at him openly. *Shit.* Without the live radio show to buffer him from the world, he felt vulnerable. He grabbed the beer that had been placed on the table by the Budweiser sales rep for marketing purposes and swallowed it in one long chug. Then, he motioned for the sales rep to get him a refill.

Maybe Amelia would fire him now. He probably deserved it.

He yanked the headphones off with the intention of taking his medicine like a man, but the minute he stood up, his path was blocked by a triad of irate female footballers. And ... at the point was the Asian beauty who'd kissed him on the stairs.

"You owe us an apology," she said.

Us. As in she played football, too? *No.* He scanned her strong but trim body, which was wrapped in a pair of painted-on jeans and a ruffled blouse that laced up over ample cleavage. Miss Saigon did not look like a football player. She didn't kiss like a football player, either.

Rome smiled.

A muscular blond with blue streaks in her hair and tattoos up the wazoo pushed in front. "And as long as we get an apology, nobody gets hurt."

"Speak for yourself," the Asian stunner said, taking the helm again and looking like she wanted a piece of him … in the most unpleasant way possible.

"Rome!" Amelia's voice rose over the madness.

He groaned. Talk about women trouble. He needed that beer. "Sorry, ladies. I'm being paged."

He turned around and came face to face with Amelia.

"Put that one on the air," she said.

Put who on the air? He turned back around and saw his stairwell kissing partner with hands on hips and challenge in her eyes.

"Hell no," came out of his mouth.

Amelia smiled. "That's not a request." She side-stepped him and addressed the women. "I'd like to offer you the opportunity to roast Rome Rizzelli live on air. What do you say?"

Seriously. Where the hell was that beer?

Chapter Three

The middle-aged woman with the headset and the sharklike smile stepped closer and smiled at Jade. "What do you have to say about that?"

She would say roasting Rome live on the air was one way to undo the mistake she'd made in the stairwell.

Nerves rattled her chest, but they were no match for the anger and adrenaline still swirling in her system after his sexist comment about getting his hands under one of those centers. *She* was a center. And there was no way in hell he was ever going to get his hands on her ... again.

"I'll do it," Jade said, glancing at the crowd in the direction where Rome had gone off, mumbling about needing another drink.

"Good! I'm Amelia London, by the way." The woman held out a hand, and Jade shook it soundly.

"I'm Jade Wren. It's nice to meet you."

"Likewise." Amelia looked at the rest of the team. "All of you. Finding out you come in after every win was a real stroke of luck, let me tell you. My father died and left me this station, and until I called this bar to set up the remote broadcast, I was beginning to think it was a cruel joke on his part. I mean, how does a proud feminist produce this show and still be able to live with herself?" She grinned. "I'll tell you how. She recognizes the opportunity to turn the industry on its head. You are that opportunity." Amelia looked right at Jade then opened her hands to the sky. "Like manna from heaven. So, come on. I'll get you outfitted with a headset, and then I can chirp in your ear the whole time. That way you won't be alone, and I won't let you look foolish. "

Just like that, the crowd parted and Rome returned with two beers in hand. Unreal. Her gaze dropped from his sour expression to his broad shoulders and over the swell of his chest, which was clearly exaggerated by his aggressive breathing. Okay, so he had a nice body and a great set of lips ... but he was definitely short.

"Fifty seconds left in the break," Amelia said with a reassuring smile. "Wait for your introduction. Then, have a normal conversation about being a women's football player. It's really that easy."

Rome was sitting again with his headphones on. He shot Jade a dismissive look, as though he suspected she didn't have the guts to do this, and her spine stiffened. Poor boy. He didn't know a damn thing about her. She'd seen that same look a million times throughout her childhood from her father, who'd always said women were weak. That look didn't intimidate her anymore; it just made her mad. It also made her want to teach its bearer a serious lesson.

She smiled back sweetly.

He looked startled. *Good.*

But the minute her thighs hit the cold seat and music filled her ears along with the familiar voiceover announcing the return of *Riled Up with Rome*, her heart leapt to her throat. He wouldn't mention the kiss, would he? *Crap.* Did this little on-air stint qualify as bad judgment?

"Well, folks, what can I say? You take a break, grab a beer, and end up with a surprise guest. And what a surprise this one is." He side-eyed Jade, and it felt a lot like a challenge. "Have we met before?"

She sat perfectly still. "Not formally. No."

He was goading her. Maybe even intimidating her. She didn't know much about radio, but she knew the kinds of things this guy did for ratings.

"Okay, then." But he gave her a look laced with knowing before he charged ahead. "My guest is Jade Wren, and apparently, she plays full tackle football for the Cleveland Clash." As he talked, his fingers flew across his laptop keyboard, and her team's website popped up. "What position?"

"Center." She sort of growled the word, and he caught on real fast.

He looked at her and smiled that sexy, cocky grin that she'd seen on the stairs. "Is that so?"

"Yes. And I promise, you won't ever get your hands under me."

Ooh! The crowd ate that up.

Amelia said, "You go, girl!" into Jade's ear. And Jade sat a little straighter.

Rome didn't seem to know what to make of it. He just navigated through the roster, until he said, "The team website says you're five eleven. Is that true?" He relaxed back in his chair and looked her over lazily from head to toe.

An unwelcomed reminder of the attraction she'd felt on the stairs heated her skin.

"I mean you're definitely ..." he paused and smiled, "leggy, but everybody knows official team stats aren't accurate. Add a couple inches here. Add ten pounds there." He looked back at the screen. "There's no way you're 160 pounds. That's a lot for a woman isn't it?"

Jerk! She opened her mouth to call him out.

"But, wait. Look at this ..." His finger rose up the roster until it hovered above Darcy Slagle's stats.

No way was Jade going to let him humiliate the heaviest player on the team.

"And how tall are *you*? About five six maybe? Isn't that short for a man?"

He dropped the shit-eating grin. In fact, he looked every bit as mortified as she felt whenever someone pointed out how freakishly tall she was for a woman. And even though she didn't want to and he didn't deserve it after the weight crack, she felt a little pang of sympathy.

"My height is irrelevant," he said, recovering quickly. "I'm not a professional athlete. Physical stature isn't part of my job description. You won't find my bodily stats on the WKST website. What's in the public domain is fair game."

True, but she doubted his comments were purely innocent athletic conjecture. "Maybe so, but I find it hard to believe you would have a Boltz player in this same seat and waste time talking about his height and weight. You would talk about skill and record."

He tilted his head, as if she'd impressed him. Or maybe he was just humoring her. "Okay, I'll bite. What's your record?"

"Six and four."

"So you're a mediocre team."

"If that's what you call a team who just advanced to the second round of playoffs." She smiled to acknowledge her teammates' thunderous cheers.

There was definitely some admiration in his gaze this time. "I stand corrected." He held up his hands, and her chest swelled with pride. "Clearly, you're in a mediocre league."

Asshole. She glowered, and sat up even straighter. "I'm beginning to think this isn't about women athletes at all. It's about women in general, isn't it? What's the matter, Rizzelli? Did a woman athlete break your heart? Did she leave you crying and all ... " It just came to her out of nowhere, and she said it with all the attitude and conviction in the world, "*Jaded?*"

"Brilliant!" Amelia raved in her ear while the crowd went wild.

Rome unleashed a slow, suggestive grin that brightened his face and sparkled in his eyes. "I like women just fine."

The words "sexist pig" came to mind, but they didn't stop the alarming hum of attraction as she stared at his lips and remembered exactly how they tasted.

"But ..." he continued, "I like my women *off the field*, if you know what I mean."

He probably liked them in the kitchen, barefoot and pregnant, too. Gag.

Jade turned in her chair to face him and leaned forward. "Oh, I'm pretty sure I do know *exactly* what you mean." Rome's eyes widened as she reached over and laid one red-lacquered nail against his chest. She lowered her voice, letting it go to just the slightest side of breathy. "I bet a guy like you likes your woman wearing some sort of sexy ..." she leaned closer, holding Rome's gaze, "red ..." closer still, licking her lips, "lace ..." she was a breath away from him now, so close she could've nearly kissed him—again, "*apron*, slaving over a hot stove while you sit on the couch scratching your ass and bellowing for her to bring you another beer."

Take that! She sat back triumphantly crossing her arms over her chest and winked at her teammates who were going crazy down in front.

Rome looked dumbfounded as he took in the crowd who was laughing *at him* instead of with him now. His face flickered with anger for a second, but then a mischievous smile stretched across his face. "Nah." He took a page from her book and leaned in, carrying with him the sinfully familiar scent of denim, soap, and beer. One whiff, and she held her breath. "No apron, sweetheart. When I'm with a lady, I don't like any distractions."

The voice in her head told her she was being played, reduced to exactly what he thought a woman was—what her father had thought a woman was: the weaker, easily managed sex. She'd spent the last six years searching for the self-confidence to prove otherwise. She'd earned a master's degree, developed a weight-lifting habit, and scored a starting position on a championship-caliber women's football team. She wasn't about to let this man or any man reduce her to a ball of quivering hormones. That kiss was officially forgotten.

Jade cracked her knuckles, like she was gearing up to snap the ball to MJ for a game-winning pass with only seconds left on the click. Rome Rizzelli wouldn't know what hit him.

• • •

Finally. Rome had reversed the course of this game, and he had her right where he wanted her. Sort of. The closer he got to her long, lean body, and the harder he looked at her sultry face, the more his libido sparked. He wouldn't mind expanding on that kiss and having her in his kitchen *and* his bed—well, if his bed wasn't in the same house where his mother and sister lived.

Roasted. As always, big bad Rome Rizzelli was full of hot air. The dude talked one hell of a game.

His rapid-fire thoughts spanned all of five seconds, but apparently that was all Jade needed to regroup. She slid her chair back an inch and set her face from sultry to guard-your-balls serious. "Have you ever even seen a women's football game?"

Amelia chuckled in his ear. "This is beautiful, Rome. I wish you could see your face."

He dismissed them both with a shrug. "Like I said before, men are faster and stronger. Why would I want to watch a substandard version of the game?"

Out of the corner of his eye, he saw some guy in an Ohio State T-shirt stagger up to the table with his hand raised. Despite being on the air, Rome gave him a high-five. His fellow Buckeyes were some of the show's biggest supporters. That had to really stick in Amelia's craw.

"Would the Buckeyes beat the Boltz?" Jade asked.

Rome felt a mix of amusement and pity. But hey, at least she was trying to have this conversation. She had no idea she was out of her league. "No chance in hell this year. If you listened to my show regularly, you would know that ..."

"The Buckeyes are six hundred pounds lighter than the Boltz on the line, a statistic that illustrates the difference between college and professional football, a statistic that supports the practice of young men not being eligible for the draft straight out of high school. And yet, you never miss an OSU game, despite the fact that statistics prove it's a substandard version of the game you love." She grinned.

Rome blinked. *Damn.* Maybe Little Miss Gridiron wasn't exactly out of her league.

He opened his mouth, but no rebuttal formed. He shook his head, but no thoughts rushed in to save him. Hell, he couldn't even remember her point. "I don't know what you're getting at."

"Of course you do," she said. "College football is not the same as professional football, but it's still football, and there's still enjoyment in watching it."

It was a tricky argument, but it wasn't foolproof. "College is one step away from the pros, and at the D-1 level, a good portion of those guys will get their shot at the NFL. How many women have a similar shot? None." *How 'bout them apples, sweetheart?*

She thought about it and then nodded. For a second, he expected her to pull out a white flag. No such luck.

"Do you enjoy high school football, Mr. Rizzelli?"

"I do."

"And how many of those young men will get their shot at the NFL? Would you say a good portion?"

He angled his body in the chair while he maintained unflinching eye contact. He didn't need a white flag. A showdown would work, too. "Depends on the school. If you're talking a powerhouse like St. Ignatius, then yes." His gaze dropped to her glossy lips as he waited on her to fire her next shot. And she would. He knew that much about her, now. She didn't stay down long. Besides, she was the type of woman who kissed strangers on her way up the steps. Why the hell *had* she kissed him anyway? He glanced at the rowdy women over Jade's shoulder and then back at Amelia. Maybe this was all part of the "Rile up Rome" plan.

"What if I'm talking about South City High School?" she asked.

"Then no." South City laid claim to one professional athlete alum, Cam Simmons, and Little Miss Gridiron knew that, didn't she? From the shadow of a grin on her pretty face, he could tell she thought she had him backed into a corner. The sexy images that accompanied that thought made him smirk. "All right, Wren, what's your point this time?"

"My point, *Rizzelli*, is your opinion is irrelevant. Since you've never been to a women's football game, you can't possibly know what you're talking about. And I'm pretty sure you'll stay away because you don't like the taste of crow."

"I don't know. I'm a hearty eater." He let her mind wander a bit, then made a face laced with superiority. "Besides, that would never happen, because I'm rarely wrong. I speak the truth. You know?"

"Oh yeah? Well, why don't you actually put your money where your mouth is this time? Come see us play." Her brown eyes twinkled in invitation.

He had no desire to go—except maybe to see her again. "I make no promises, Wren. I'm a busy man."

But from the smile that dug into his face, he knew the odds were in her favor.

Chapter Four

Monday morning, Jade was up and ready for the last week of math camp, which she taught in the summers from 11:00 a.m. until 4:00 p.m. at Sunrise Academy, where she was the full-time enrichment teacher during the school year. As she poured herself one final cup of coffee in the kitchen of her small two-bedroom apartment in South City, she glanced at the clock. *10:00 a.m.*

She absolutely, positively forbade herself to turn on *Riled Up with Rome.* It was bad enough she couldn't seem to shed the adrenaline from Saturday night. She'd spent the rest of the weekend going over every word, every volley, every look in her head. And that kiss, the kiss that was supposed to have been forgotten. Easier said than done.

She sighed, slammed the pot back onto the warmer, and lamented how even her teammates had commented on the chemistry between them.

She did not want to have chemistry with Rome. The guy was a jerk. No lopsided, sexy-as-sin grin and magical green eyes could change that. Plus, he was short, short, short. Not exactly the five six she'd accused him of, but quite possibly shorter than her. Five eight? Five nine? She didn't want to even think about how close they would have to be again for her to know for sure. All she needed to think about was that she did not do short guys—in any way, shape, or form.

And yet, here she was with her finger hovering over the radio app on her phone. This was going to require a serious pep talk.

If you open it, it's double burpees tonight. Her finger didn't retreat at the thought. *Make that triple.* She hated squat thrusts only slightly more than she hated planks, but she wasn't above doing enough to make her collapse just to excise this demon.

Finally, she shoved her phone into her duffle bag. *Good girl.*

But when she made it to her car and started the ignition, the radio kicked on like it always did, and Rome's voice greeted her.

"It's 10:15 a.m., for crying out loud! Wake up, people."

Shut him off. She reached for the power button.

"If you really think a former D-2 offensive line coach is going to make that much of a difference on the Boltz's upcoming season, you need to go back to bed and stop taking the damn sleeping pills, because you're talking in your sleep."

Jade dropped her hand. The Boltz hired another line coach? Who? She'd heard about Jay McAllister joining the coaching staff, but he'd been the offensive coordinator at Colorado State --Pueblo. Which was D-2. She listened closely, because a swell of excitement told her she was about to catch Rome in a mistake.

"McAllister doesn't have the experience to make a big impact."

Bingo. "McAllister was the OC at Colorado, you idiot!" Her laughter mixed with Rome rattling off the station's call-in number. She should call. Correct him live on air. He would hate that. A swell of excitement bowled her over like a title wave. What had gotten into her? Whatever it was, it was powerful, so powerful she pulled onto the side of the road and fished her phone from her bag.

Quick! Do it before somebody else does. Her fingers raced clumsily over the screen even as she told herself this was crazy, and he might not take her call.

"Hello!" It was a woman's voice. "Thanks for calling Sports Radio 94.7. Who would you like to talk to, and what is the topic you're calling about?"

Jade's heart rate spiked. She took a quick, fortifying breath, turned off her car radio, and said, "I'd like to talk to Rome Rizzelli. He just said Jay McAllister was an offensive line coach at Colorado State-Pueblo, and that's wrong. I'd like to correct him."

"Name?"

"Jade Wren."

"Okay. I'll put you through. Wait for Rome to say your name before speaking."

Yes! She gave the steering wheel a victorious smack.

After a few seconds of silence and then a dull click, she heard voices again. Rome and another caller where talking about the Boltz's first-round draft pick, who was recently arrested on drug charges.

"Let the guy play until the league says otherwise," the caller said. "Innocent until proven guilty."

Rome blew a loud raspberry. "Thanks for calling, Mack, but you're a total jackass. This guy was trouble in college. He's going to be trouble in the pros. Management needs to come down hard and come down fast, unless they want another Gordon. And that's the truth. You don't like it, you can Rome your ass out of here." Jade rolled her eyes, and that annoying horn rang in her ear so loudly she almost didn't hear him say her name. "Jade in South City, that's a very interesting name. I met a Jade once ... on a set of stairs. It was a very inspired meeting. You wouldn't happen to be her, would you?"

He was so unprofessional. She squared her shoulders and sniffed back the alarm at having him skirt around the kiss live on the air. "No. I'm the Jade who roasted your ass on Saturday night. Remember me?"

"How could I forget?" He sounded annoyed, and that gave her endless satisfaction, so did knowing where she was heading with this call. "But I'm not calling to rehash Saturday night. I'm calling to correct you on Jay McAllister. You said he was an offensive line coach at Colorado State-Pueblo, but he was actually the offensive coordinator." She let that settle with a smile on her face. His fingers were probably frantically calling up Google.

"No. I'm pretty sure you're wrong about that."

"Look it up."

"I am." She waited patiently with her heart racing out of her chest, then she heard him say, "If you're wrong, will you stop badgering me? It's starting to feel a little stalker-like."

She laughed, even though she tried not to. "Sure. But if I'm right, you have to come see a Cleveland Clash playoff game."

He was quiet a beat too long, and then he spoke up, sounding pained. "Folks, I stand corrected. Jay McAllister was indeed the OC at Colorado State-Pueblo, but ..." he hurried up, "that doesn't change the point I was trying to make. McAllister was a sub-par hire." Another pause was followed by a loud exhalation. "Thanks *so* much for bringing that to my attention, Jade." The sarcasm boosted her ego.

"You're welcome. I'll see you on Saturday at the game."

"I never agreed to that."

"Kickoff is at 7:00 p.m. at Heisman Stadium. Tickets can be purchased online or at the gates."

"You're going to make me pay for a ticket?"

"No, I just wanted to plug my team and invite your listeners. I'll leave your ticket at Will Call."

"Touché, Wren." She could've sworn she'd heard him chuckle. "I may or may not see you there."

"Oh, you'll be there. You wouldn't want your fans to think you're just full of hot air, now would you?"

Jade was still smiling when she walked into Sunrise Academy fifteen minutes later. What a rush! This whole coming out of your shell and not letting fear rule your life thing was worth every nervous flutter and upset stomach. Between making it to the playoffs, benching her personal best last night, and two successful "appearances" on *Riled Up with Rome*, she felt invincible. Capable of doing and having anything. A force to be reckoned with. The top ...

"Jade, can I see you in my office?" Laurel Moses, the principal, rushed a wobbly smile and then spun on her thick-soled, black pumps and headed for the open door.

All the pumped-up emotions Jade had been feeling a second ago deflated instantly, nerves suddenly churning in the deepest pit of her stomach and making her queasy. No matter how old she got, no matter how high the GPA that went along with her teaching degree, getting called to the principal's office sucked. Maybe something was wrong with one of her summer camp students. Hopefully not. Then again, maybe a parent had complained about her passing out freeze pops after math tag last week. Between the artificial colors and high sugar content, it was a real possibility. But come on! It had been ninety degrees! She hated dealing with ornery parents even more than she hated dealing with ornery kids.

Laurel closed the door and walked behind the desk, where she didn't take a seat. The standing made Jade even more nervous. Something bad had happened. She could feel it.

"Jade, I have some news about the coming school year. The gifted program is being cut."

She heard the words. On some level, she even understood them enough to form a couple important questions in her head: Where did that leave the dedicated enrichment teacher? What about her math camp? But she was worried and shocked enough to stay quiet.

"We're putting enrichment back into the hands of the general classroom teachers rather than offering it as a special, separate curriculum. And unfortunately, we don't have any in-classroom openings, which means we can't shuffle you into a full-time general teaching position."

"Crap."

"I'm sorry, Jade. We tried everything to balance the budget without losing any programs. Art is being cut, too. Music is going half-time. This has nothing to do with performance or capabilities. I promise you that. And the good news is you're eligible for unemployment."

Crap! Crap! Crap! Unemployment would pay merely a portion of her measly salary. A portion that would not be enough to pay her expenses, including car payment and rent, especially now that Jillian was engaged and on the verge of moving out.

"I'm sure you have questions," Laurel said.

She should, but she sat there stunned and oddly embarrassed, like somehow it was her fault. Her mother and grandmother were going to be so disappointed.

She did not want to deal with this right now. "Thank you for letting me know, but can we talk about this later? I really need to get the room set up before the kids get here."

"Of course, and again, I'm so sorry."

Jade nodded. "Me too."

Now what? She tried to come up with a plan as she walked down the long, air-conditioned hallway. It was almost July. New grads had been applying and interviewing for open, fall teaching positions around the city since May. Was anything left in other private schools or public districts?

Do not panic. Worst-case scenario, she could wait tables at Tanya's mother's restaurant, which was right downstairs from her apartment. Or maybe she should say worst-case scenario, she could move back home with Umma and Halmoni.

God no. That was not an option. Not that she didn't love and need them, but these last six months of a little physical separation had been good for her. She was finally formulating her own opinions about the world and finding her own voice. She wanted to keep that momentum.

Jade stayed positive for the rest of the day, focusing on the kids and their fantasy baseball team project that would take them through to the end of the week. When the last "camper" had been picked up and she was free to go, she bypassed Laurel's office and headed home. No use beating a dead horse and all that. Besides, she needed to switch gears and put the job worry behind her. Including tonight's practice, the Clash only had five days to get ready to face New York. A win on Saturday meant they'd be headed to the championship! Talk about a boost to her mood.

After a quick stop at her apartment for a protein bar and her duffle bag, Jade drove out to John Heisman Stadium. She was three steps from her car when Jillian and her fiancé, Carter, pulled in and parked. Loud bass music reverberated from inside Carter's luxury car, and despite the tinted windows, Jade could see that they were laughing about something. *Cute.* Even as she said it, a pang of jealousy hit her square in the chest. She didn't think she would ever have something like that. She couldn't seem to let her guard down long enough to find it. Seeing a man hit a woman was the perfect anti-aphrodisiac. And her ensuing reluctance to get involved with anyone was exactly the reason why her mother and grandmother had taken the lead.

Jillian popped out of the car and waved. "What's up, sistah?"

"I don't have a job this fall."

"No!" she shrieked dramatically. "Why?"

"As soon as math camp ends, I'm officially unemployed thanks to budget cuts."

"What's all the yelling about?" Carter, who was part of the Clash's coaching staff, flashed a wicked smile and slammed his car door.

"Jade was fired," Jillian said.

"Laid off." She was a damn good teacher, thank you very much.

"Tough break," Carter said.

What else could she do but nod?

Jillian tossed an arm around Jade's shoulders. "You'll find something else. Don't sweat it. And don't let it get in your head and screw up your game."

"No way." She reached up and squeezed Jillian's hand. "I'm not going to talk about it again until we kick New York's ass."

She was just about to tell them about what had happened with Rome that morning when her phone rang. It buzzed against her hipbone with a call from her mother. "I'm not going to answer that. I'll call her later." And she'd probably get suckered into talking about her job status, too, which would be a huge disappointment to her mother, who had gleefully paid tuition bills with the belief that teaching was a stable, secure profession, perfect for a wife and mother.

"Maybe she has another Korean boy to fix you up with." Jillian bobbed her brows. "Did you meet the tall one yet?"

"No, he's still out of town."

"This is where I bow out," Carter said. "See you on the field, ladies."

Jade's phone rang again. She fully expected it to be her relentless mother. But this time, it was a blocked caller. For some reason, that made her the slightest bit nervous. She didn't answer it, and three steps inside the locker room, her phone buzzed again, signaling a new voice mail. *That* was probably her mother rattling on about some gossip she'd heard at the beauty shop she owned and operated in the heart of Koreatown, Cleveland, or like Jillian had said, offering up another Korean boy. Jade had nothing against Asian men. She just hated the incessant need to see her married off and "happy."

She flashed the phone at Jillian. "Do I want to listen to this before practice?"

"Yes, you do. It'll frustrate the hell out of you, and then you can use it to tear up the field." She grinned. "You can thank me later."

That was a good way to look at it. Jade hit the play button and brought the phone to her ear. However, the female voice didn't belong to her mother.

"Jade, this is Amelia London from Sports Radio 94.7. If you could call me back when you have a few minutes, I'd appreciate it. I'd like to talk to you about a job opportunity."

Wide-eyed and a little breathless at the end of the voice mail, Jade listened to it again.

"What's up?" Jillian asked.

"I'm not sure, but how's this for crazy? I think Amelia London's about to offer me a job in sports radio."

Chapter Five

Game day. Just not exactly a game Rome had ever expected to be watching.

He climbed the bleacher steps at John Heisman Stadium under the sweltering Saturday afternoon sun, having refused to talk his way into the air-conditioned press box, even though it probably wouldn't have taken much. Because this was not an "official" visit, and he didn't want anyone getting the wrong idea.

WKST was not covering women's sports. *Rome Rizzelli* was not covering women's sports. No matter what Amelia said.

As he climbed, a few people called out to him. He wasn't recognized that often since it was radio, but apparently, his reputation here proceeded him. Which was good and bad. He never knew how to act in public when he was off duty. The people who knew him from the show probably expected the same brash treatment, but Rome did his best to leave that guy at the station. There was certainly no room for shock jock antics at home.

"You covering the game, Rome?" a chubby guy in an Indians jersey and a Boltz cap asked as Rome passed.

"Nope. I'm just curious." Which was the honest to God truth.

"He lost a bet!" yelled out the short guy behind him. "Ain't that right, Rome?"

Rome entertained the man with a chuckle. "It seems that way."

That's why there'd been a single ticket waiting from him at Will Call. He thought about leaving it there and buying his own, just to keep her guessing about whether or not he'd been here, but in the end, he wanted her to know he came. That he came to see *her*. Women's football didn't interest him for any other reason.

And from the looks of the stands, women's football didn't interest most people. For a divisional championship game, the attendance was weak except for a thick pocket of a hundred or so noisy fans on the fifty-yard line. Everywhere else, the crowd was spotty. Even a D-3 college team would fill this place. Hell, he'd been to high school playoff games here, and it had been standing room only. This did not bode well for the caliber of the game he was about to see.

He walked down an empty Row K to Seat 11 and propped his feet onto the metal bench in front of him. With his elbows resting on his knees, he took in the on-field activity.

Both teams were scattered and moving through seemingly random pregame rituals. Some stretched. Some passed. Some worked on footwork. But a good number of them lingered on the sidelines. At first glance, from up here, he wouldn't have immediately suspected they were women, save for the inordinate amount of ponytails. Not that guys like Polamalu and Matthews hadn't put long hair on the NFL map ages ago. Still … those guys weren't shaped like this. More specifically, they didn't have boobs. Even shoulder pads couldn't completely mask a few sets on this field. And hips. His gaze roved the crowd for one pair of hips in particular, and his right hand unconsciously flexed.

He zeroed in on a woman crouching on the sideline in what looked like a makeshift gauntlet drill. A long, black ponytail spilled down her back, splitting the number sixty. There was precision and elegance in her posture and a sneaky beauty in the bend of her backside and fold of her thighs. *Jade.* He would have recognized her even if he hadn't looked up her number on the team roster already.

The longer he looked and the closer he studied her, the creepier he felt. No matter how much he told himself this was just another sporting event and she was just another athlete, he couldn't keep himself from concentrating on other things … like the fact that those football pants hugged her hips like an environmentalist at a Redwood tree cutting.

That was not going to work. This was football. Rate her speed, her strength, and her hands, he told himself. Watch how she handles the nose tackle, not how she crouches low and bounces fast in a deep squat that proved impressive flexibility and had his mouth dry even though the rest of him was sweating.

He wiped a clammy hand across his forehead. Maybe he should find some shade after all. The sun was obviously messing with him. But before he could move again, music poured from the overhead speakers, followed by the announcer's welcome.

The stadium slowly but steadily filled with more people until Rome had company in his row—a couple senior citizens wearing floppy sun hats. That was about the pace he expected from a women's football game. Add to that the fact that the kickoff by the opposing team was weak and wobbly, and he was pretty sure he'd be bailing at the half.

But then number 60 took the field, and he tried not to look enthralled by the long, lean strides and the curve of her crouch. When his view of her was blocked by the surprisingly hefty defensive line, he swore under his breath. Not that he needed to be obsessing over her.

Wham! Out of nowhere, the first-down play was underway with a quick snap to the quarterback who was under center. It reminded him of his comment Saturday night about how he'd like to get his "hands under one of those centers." Yeah, that had been pretty ridiculous. Jade had gone on to rightfully put him in his place, but if he ever got a chance to talk to her privately one of these days, he would definitely give her the apology she deserved.

In a blink, she barreled off the line and pancaked the nose tackle. Rome would've whistled if he wasn't already laughing. *Damn.* It took oxlike strength to land a block like that. He was honestly surprised a woman could do that. Sure, she'd done it to another woman, but he bet if he looked up the tackle's stats, he'd see she was over two hundred pounds. Ounce for ounce, that was impressive. So was the whizzing ball that caught his eye. It soared an easy thirty yards in a perfect spiral. The QB had an admirable arm. Add it to the list of surprises. He suddenly had a feeling this day would be full of them.

Not long after, Rome got his chance to whistle when the wide receiver caught a ball in full coverage like it was on a zip line. With pressure breathing down her neck from the back and right, she sprinted a tightrope along the sideline before she leaped a defender at the one-yard line and tumbled into the end zone. *Strike hard. Strike fast.*

Impressive.

The old couple beside him jumped to their feet, clapping and dancing to some electro-pop music that livened up the crowd. Rome stayed seated.

"You for New York?" the old guy asked.

Rome shook his head. "Nope."

"You're not cheering," the old woman said.

"I'm impartial."

But he knew he wasn't as he homed in on Jade on the sideline and his interest piqued. Pretty, witty, and athletic. He didn't think they made women like that. Then again, his experience had been tainted by too many remote shows in trashy bars where inebriated young things offered him everything and anything from weed to blow jobs the minute his headphones came off. That was sort of what he'd expected from her when she'd kissed him on the stairs actually. But he'd been wrong. This woman clearly wasn't impressed with Rome Rizzelli.

Maybe that was part of the allure.

New York fumbled, and he sat a little straighter, knowing Jade would be back on the line. But the Clash went three and out after some yawn-inducing running plays, and he was back to creeping on Jade while she stood on the sideline.

"That's my granddaughter!" the old guy said, when New York's quarterback ended up on her ass. "Number fifty. She leads the league in sacks."

Rome nodded. Now the old guy's enthusiasm made sense. In fact, this stadium was probably filled with friends and family, not necessarily just fans of the game. But as Rome watched the Clash quarterback launch another bomb, he thought the lack of public support was a bit of a shame. Were they perfect? Hardly. But he had to give Jade props. She'd been right on target with her analogy about high school vs. college vs. pro football. They all had their draws, and he supposed women's football was no different.

Again, he found himself staring at Jade. Maybe he would talk to her after the game ... offer to buy her a drink ... find out what it would take to impress her the way she'd impressed him.

• • •

Jade was only in this bar on a postgame Saturday night for three reasons. One: Rome said "a drink." How painful could one drink be? Two: She wanted to watch him eat crow after the Clash had beaten New York 21-10 and advanced to the conference championship earlier that day. And three: Four days ago, Amelia had offered her a job that involved sharing airtime with Rome. Before Jade walked into that radio station, she ought to get to know the guy a little better, especially since they'd sort of started off on the wrong foot.

Memories of that damn kiss reared their ugly head again. She was nervous enough about his reaction to working with her after everything that had gone down. She glanced at the empty seat across from her, tempted to hightail it out of there but resigned herself to waiting to hear his opinion.

She supposed it was only fair since she'd already made him wait for this drink until after she'd gone for celebratory ice cream with Umma and Halmoni and had promised them tonight she would be a *good girl*. Now, Rome was the one making her wait, having left the bar to take a phone call seconds after he'd walked in wearing what she was starting to think was his uniform—worn jeans, white T-shirt beneath an untucked button-down, and that crooked smile that advertised all sorts of trouble.

As much as she hated to play by her mother and grandmother's rules on a Saturday night when they weren't around, "good girls" did not need trouble.

When Rome returned to the bar, the air of trouble that accompanied his swagger blasted her hard in the face, taking her breath away. *Judgment do not fail me now.*

He slapped his phone on the high-top table with an aggressiveness that made her internal alarm sirens blare. It looked like the guy had a quick temper, just like her dad.

"Sorry about that," Rome said. "If it's not one thing, it's another." He glanced at his phone and made a face. "Has the waitress been by? I could really use that drink."

More sirens, especially when she thought back to the beer he'd been drinking during the show. Jade shook her head. "Not yet."

He fisted his hand and pounded it lightly but soundly on the table.

"Is everything okay?" she asked. Maybe if she got him talking about it, he would settle down. Then, she could get on with what she really came for and get out of here.

He shook his head, but then his phone buzzed against the table, and she caught the name of the caller before he snatched it up. *Mom.*

Instead of answering it, he shoved the phone in his back pocket and sat.

As odd and inappropriate as it was, she smiled. "Do we have the same mother?"

His brow crooked in curiosity. "Why? Is your mother convinced you're trying to kill her because you lock up her Vicodin when you leave the house?"

Ouch. That wasn't exactly the friendly, calming getting-to-know-you conversation starter she'd had in mind. "No. I just meant my mother calls all the time, too."

"Sorry." He roughed a palm across his face and then offered a quick smile. "It just gets old sometimes. But the worry never does."

She bet.

"Why does your mom call all the time?" he asked, swiftly changing the subject.

"Well ..." It was embarrassing, but not nearly as embarrassing as admitting your mother was addicted to prescription meds, "she wants me to have the perfect life, which is something she didn't have, and in her mind, the perfect life includes a stable job and a nice Korean guy. She wants to find me one of those real quick—before I go off and find a horrible American guy on my own and ruin everything." She laughed, because it sounded so ridiculous.

Again, Rome's brow rose, followed by a sly smile that had her squirming. This was where they would talk about the kiss once and for all, wasn't it? Maybe she should beat him to it. But as she opened her mouth to tackle the topic, the waitress showed up.

They spent the next minute or two distracted by drink and appetizer orders. Yes, "just one drink" didn't involve a platter of nachos, but she had to eat. And when the waitress left, the impulse to mention the kiss had left with her. In fact, Jade figured she was off the hook as far as the horrible American guy comment went, too.

She should've known better. After all, this was Rome Rizzelli. The guy lived to make people squirm.

"So am I to assume there's a long list of horrible American guys in your past?" He looked news-anchor serious for a second, but then he grinned.

As nervous as he made her, that grin was disarming.

"Not a long one." Only three. Kyle, the boozer; her high school boyfriend, the cheater; and her father.

Something on her face must've given away her discomfort, because after a quick knowing look, he changed the subject as deftly as he'd changed it when they'd been talking about his mother. "Congratulations on the win."

Now, *this* was what she'd come for. She sat a little straighter and lifted her chin. "Thank you. Not too shabby, huh?"

"Better than I expected."

"Oh, please. You didn't expect much. We had to have blown those expectations out of the water."

There was a smug glint in his eye. "Let's just say, after seeing that, I'm pretty confident your team could beat South City High School." He winked, and that softened the blow of his less-than-complimentary underlying meaning.

"South City went completely defeated last year. I'm pretty sure we would destroy them."

"I should try to arrange that showdown, because I'd pay to see you pancake some cocky seventeen-year-old."

His smirk said he'd seen her take New York's nose tackle by surprise, and he was impressed. She liked that. "Considering I'm twenty-six, that might be illegal somehow."

"Probably, but it would be worth it." He laughed. The rich sound proved as disarming as his smile.

This did not seem like the Rome Rizzelli she'd been listening to for the last four months, the man who was loud and obnoxious on air.

The waitress returned with the draft craft beer Rome had ordered and a bottle of Michelob Ultra for Jade.

"Do you want a glass?" the gruff woman asked.

"Nope. This is good."

"I'll be right back with your nachos."

When they were alone again, Rome sipped the creamy foam off the top of his beer with his eyes lingering on Jade. She tipped her bottle back and looked away. Being here with him was ... strange. And they still hadn't broached the subject of the job offer ... or the kiss. Maybe he was okay with the idea of working with her. Maybe this invitation was because of the offer. She didn't want to believe it had anything to do with that kiss.

"You drink beer from the bottle." He set his glass down and studied her more intently.

She had a feeling she knew what he was getting at. "Yep. Is there a problem with that?"

"No. Not at all."

"Oh, come on." She tipped back the bottle again and let it linger at her lips before taking a long pull and then a slow lick of her lips. "You think it's weird for a woman to drink out of a bottle, just like you think it's weird for a woman to play football. I've been listening to you for months. You have a lot of sexist ideas. You know?"

He looked a little shell shocked as he watched her lick her lips. "Actually, a lot of that is a put on. Most of it. I go as big and as bold as I can to get a reaction on the air." He narrowed his eyes slightly, thoughtfully. "Remember that comment about wanting to get my hands under a center?"

She wrinkled her face. "How could I forget?"

"I'm sorry. That was really rude. Had I known anything about you at the time or that you were coming on air, I never would've gone that far." He looked sincere, but she didn't know what to believe. "It's like there are two sides of me," he continued. "On air and off. That probably sounds strange."

Maybe not. Maybe it was kind of like acting or reality TV. And in a way, she could relate to the whole having two sides thing. The Jade her mother and grandmother knew was nothing like the Jade she had come to be.

When she didn't say anything, he blinked and settled back in his seat. "You know, when my father was alive, he loved that my mother drank beer from the bottle. He once told me that's how he knew she'd be both his friend and, well, more than a friend." He looked away. "That probably sounded even stranger than the two sides comment, huh?"

No. It was actually kind of sweet, and she found herself even more interested in the idea that there was a different man behind the on-air personality. "How long ago did your father die?"

"Thirteen years ago. A massive heart attack took him in his sleep. Man, it's been a rough road ever since."

She thought about his mother again, and she felt inexplicably sad. Did the woman's addiction have anything to do with losing her husband? But that seemed like too intimate a question to ask of a coworker.

"Why did you kiss me on the steps?" He levied the random question without warning or discomfort, taking her off guard.

Talk about intimate. "Um, well, I was trying to prove a point."

"To?"

"Myself." *My mother.* Both.

He dropped his elbows to the table and leaned closer as her cheeks heated the slightest bit. "And what was the point you were trying to prove?"

She swallowed an extra-large gulp of beer. "I was trying to prove to myself that I can take certain risks without anything bad happening."

Rome tipped his beer to his lips but, instead of drinking, grinned. "Was that what you were trying to do when you approached my table during break? Take a risk? Prove a point to yourself?"

She made a face. "No, I was trying to prove one to you ... that you don't always know what you're talking about."

He laughed. But there was no laughing five minutes later when their hands brushed atop a heaping plate of nachos while they discussed how their back-and-forth broadcast on Saturday night had probably made for good radio. In fact, the soft, incidental contact on the outside of her hand left a burn that lingered, and the longer it lingered, the more it bothered her. But was that reason enough to second-guess taking this job?

Nope. Absolutely not. She simply set her hands in her lap and reeled in the ambiguity. The kiss had been a mistake, and it would not happen again, especially now that she had a name to go with the lips.

Two more sips of her beer amid conversation that had turned back to the Clash's win, and she reached the bottom. Then, she placed her bottle soundly on the table, because it was time to talk about Amelia's job offer and then go.

Rome eyed her up suspiciously and asked, "Am I keeping you from something? Maybe a horrible American man?"

At the moment, he was the only horrible American man she was worried about ... because in this setting, he didn't seem quite so horrible.

"Actually, I'm meeting up with my team after this."

He nodded.

"You did say one drink." She lifted her empty bottle and smiled.

He didn't smile back. "Maybe next time I can convince you to have two ... or three." There was a heat in his emerald eyes that she tried desperately to ignore.

"I never have more than two," she said.

"Then two it will be."

She shook her head, but smiled to soften the blow. "I don't think drinking together and getting overly friendly is a good idea for coworkers. Do you?"

"Coworkers?" His eyes widened. "What the hell are you talking about?"

•••

Amelia had gone behind his back and hired Jade? *Helllll no.* Here he'd been thinking this evening was going well, what with all her flirting and lollipopping that bottle of beer. She'd seemed genuinely interested in him, but she was only interested in his job. Like he didn't already have enough trouble on that front.

"I haven't signed anything yet, so technically it's not official," she stammered. "I was assuming you knew."

"Do I look like I knew?"

"No."

They were done here. He scanned the crowd for the waitress, eager to get the bill. Maybe he should make Jade pay for her half, since she was going to end up costing him plenty. "Was this the plan all along?"

"The plan? No. There's no plan. Amelia's offer surprised me, too."

He wasn't buying it. The random meeting on the stairway at Ballers'. The seductive kiss. The confrontation at his table during the break, and then Amelia having the big idea of putting Jade on the air. If you asked him, it was all too convenient. Like an elaborate setup.

He caught the waitress's eye and motioned for the check.

"Amelia said after hearing us together on Saturday night, she wanted to do something to really shake up the airwaves and bring in more female listeners. She thinks a few segments a week targeting women could go a long way toward boosting ratings." Jade picked at the nachos while she spoke, pulling the jalapeños off each chip before she took a bite. It was a quirk he'd noticed earlier and had thought was cute. Not anymore. He refused to be sidetracked by silly food habits and tight pants when his job was under attack.

But then she held his gaze, and somehow her words seeped in. He had to admit—again—that they'd been good together on Saturday night. Did she annoy him? Yes. At first. Especially when the crowd had been on her side. But eventually, the mutual teasing had given way to something more, something fun. Spending a few segments a week repeating that actually wasn't a terrible way to do Amelia's bidding.

As long as this wasn't some covert operation to rid him of his job.

"Amelia said a few segments a week, right?" he asked. "She actually used the word segments?"

"Yes," Jade said. "She said segments."

Segments were no more than overglorified guest appearances. Fifteen to twenty minutes at the most. Like bringing in a weather or traffic girl.

"And it's temporary," she rushed. "Until I find a teaching position. I'm a teacher, not a radio show host. Or I was. I was laid off because of budget cuts." She shrugged, a frown marring her pretty face. "I just thought this would be a more interesting, enjoyable way to pay the bills than waiting tables. Something outside my comfort zone. I like to push myself. Prove points." She backed that up with a shaky smile. "Amelia knows I'm not staying."

He relaxed the slightest bit. His job was still on the line, but it no longer seemed like his replacement had been handpicked. He was sure enough of that, he didn't rush to pay the bill when the waitress brought the check. Instead, he refocused on Jade. "So you're a teacher, huh?"

She nodded. "Math with a master's degree in gifted education."

He whistled. Not only was she beautiful and athletic, she was book smart, too. Yeah, sharing a booth with her a few times a week wouldn't be a hardship. "You know what this means?"

She shook her head.

"You definitely owe me two drinks next time. Consider it payback for weaseling into my professional space."

Her shaky smile turned saucy. "But then wouldn't I be weaseling into your *personal* space?"

He grinned. "I sure as hell hope so."

Chapter Six

Tuesday was day two of training at WKST, and Jade was over-whelmed. Give her probability and statistics, and watch her soar. Tell her she had to write her own material for three fifteen-minute segments a week, and watch her crumble.

"Where do I get my ideas?" she asked Amelia, who'd been painfully patient.

"Wake up early to read the newspaper, hit the major sporting news sites, and watch ESPN. When you see something that makes you comment in your head, run with it."

"It's not rocket science," added a gravelly voice.

Jade looked up to find Rome, who'd been on air for the last four hours, standing in the doorway. Tousled hair, crooked smile, and a steady gaze in her direction.

"At this rate, she'll never be ready." He narrowed his eyes at Amelia, but then winked at Jade.

"I'll be ready," she countered.

"Good." His slow, sexy smile charged the air between them. "I'm getting tired of waiting."

Did he intend it to have a double meaning?

He disappeared down the hall, and Amelia faced her. "Be careful around him. He talks a good game, but I'm not buying the generous host act. If he gives you trouble, you tell me. There are actions I can take."

Geez. From the beginning, Jade could sense there was no love lost between Amelia and Rome, but hearing the station owner talk about her top talent like he was more trouble than he was worth reminded Jade that she needed to be extra careful not to get stuck in the middle of station politics.

"Okay," she said, offering Amelia a reassuring smile.

"Good. I have a meeting in ten minutes, so why don't you use one of the computers in the break room to get some ideas for a sample segment? When I'm done with my call, we'll practice in an open studio."

Jade headed for the break room amid a swarm of ambivalence. Teaching was so much easier. A classroom filled with kids was happy and safe. It also happened to be where her mother wanted her to be. Umma hadn't spent seven days a week cutting every head in Koreatown to pay college tuition just so she could watch Jade turn her back on two degrees.

Guilt set up like heartburn in her chest. Hopefully she'd get a call about a teaching position soon.

"Hey! Where are you going?"

It was Rome, again. He popped out from a room she'd passed and fell into step beside her.

"To the break room." She glanced at him. *Down* at him. She'd worn a decent wedge today. The strappy shoes matched her maxi dress. But they also served as a much-needed reminder that no matter what had happened on the steps at Ballers' and no matter the wonky attraction that seemed to be lingering between them, Rome's height was a deal breaker.

Amelia had nothing to worry about.

"Care if I join you?" he asked.

She glanced at him again, and even though that crooked smile shot a thrill right through her, she shrugged noncommittally. "Sure."

He stopped at the break room door, letting her go first. It wasn't necessarily polite. It could've simply been coincidence. In fact, he was probably checking out her ass.

She looked over her shoulder and saw him huddled by the coffeepot instead.

"What's your poison?" he asked, raising an empty mug. "Coffee, tea, soda? Sadly, there's no bottled beer here." But there was a sparkle in his eyes.

"I'm, uh, nothing. I have some research to do." She pulled out a chair and sat behind a computer, but instead of getting busy, she watched the muscles in his forearms flex as he filled his mug.

"Did Amelia give you an assignment?" he asked.

"She told me to come up with a sample segment."

"Would you like some help?" He strolled across the room until he was standing beside her.

She looked up at him and tried to decide. He didn't look short, now. In fact, he looked a lot like he'd looked on the steps moments before she'd kissed him. But looks were definitely deceiving. "Thanks, but I'm good," she said. "I'm sure you have your own work to do."

He shook his head and pulled up a chair. "I'm free for a little bit, so let me show you how it's done."

It was a terrible idea, because it involved him leaning in and reaching across her to access the keyboard. He smelled like laundry soap and soft flannel, and she had to fight the urge to turn her head for a better whiff.

She stared mindlessly at the bright and busy screen as ESPN. com flickered scores and headlines.

"The most important advice I can give you is that everybody's going to be talking about the same damn thing, so it's up to you to put your spin on it." He reached across her again, this time for the mouse, and she held her breath. "People don't listen to sports radio for breaking news. They listen for the opinions. You have to have an opinion. Good or bad. The opinion gets you listeners. Whether they love or hate you doesn't matter. What matters is whether or not they're listening. If they're listening, you'll keep your job. Got it?"

"Yep." He seemed to be the poster child for that.

"Like this, for instance." Again, he reached beyond her. This time, she gave up the struggle and just enjoyed the scent. "Mason Tennell, who's a D-1 running back, is in trouble for selling autographs, which we both know is a big no-no, because college athletes are nonpro. They shouldn't be making any money off the game."

"So the university can make millions," Jade said sarcastically.

"Look at you," Rome said with a bright smile on his face. "That's exactly what I was talking about when I said have an opinion. Now, you just expand on it. Let yourself get carried away."

It was just a few seconds really, a brief period of happy eye contact being levied from mere inches away, but it got to her. She felt the smile fade from her face much the same as it faded from his. And then she made the mistake of remembering that kiss. Maybe he was remembering, too, because his gaze dropped to her lips.

"Rizzelli!"

Jade bolted to attention. Some guy she hadn't seen before stood in the doorway.

"Amelia is on the warpath over some voiceovers. She told me to find your ass and drag it in."

Rome stood with a sigh. "Of course she is. No dragging necessary." But he did swipe a hand across Jade's shoulder as he turned to leave. "Good luck with the piece."

The contact was unsettling, because it felt good. And she knew better than to trust that. She didn't know him enough to believe he was a truly decent guy 100 percent of the time he was off air. Amelia certainly didn't seem to think so.

The longer she sat there staring at the screen, the sillier she felt. It was all neither here nor there. She had absolutely nothing to worry about. Deep down, she was the *good girl* her mother and grandmother had raised. And while she knew how to have fun and break loose now and then, she'd never met a man who could make her forget how ugly relationships could be.

•••

"Hold up. You want to what?" Rome stared in disbelief at Amelia, who'd strolled into his office later that afternoon to drop another bomb.

"Introducing Jade to listeners during a remote segment will create an even bigger buzz. And if it catches on, we'll do these segments regularly. We'll call them Man vs. Woman, which is genius if you ask me."

It was taking things a little too far if you asked him, but who was he to speak out against pushing the envelope? Besides, Amelia's word was gospel around here.

"How are you at weight lifting?" she asked.

Did carrying his near-invalid mother around the house count? Because he hadn't lifted an actual weight since college. "What does that have to do with anything?"

"Our first segment is a lift off. Jade vs. Rome."

Oh, hell. Images of the nose tackle she'd pancaked filled his head. He was strong, but was he that strong?

"Jade's a hobby bodybuilder," Amelia said with an evil grin. "Might want to practice your technique."

"Why? It's radio, not television. Nobody's going to see me."

"I'm starting a YouTube channel for the station. Bonus content that listeners can access through our site. Brilliant!" She laughed as she left his office.

"It's crazy!" He slammed the door behind her.

If Barry Vincent didn't own the only other sports radio station in town, he would've started floating résumés already. But honestly, the thought of all that upheaval. Changing health insurance possibly. Waiting for new pay periods to kick in. He knew he was staying. He sure as hell didn't want to uproot his family the way Glenn was having to.

Rome walked to his desk to flip open his laptop and Google "weight-lifting tips and tricks."

He was screwed.

Two days later, when he walked into a dingy boxing gym in South City and laid eyes on Jade in a pair of black spandex shorts that rode her rock-hard ass and a hot-pink sports bra that showed off every inch of bronze, toned skin, being screwed didn't seem like such a bad thing. He'd never seen a body that sleek and strong up close and personal before.

Normally, Rome went for short and curvy. Comfortable. Because as interested as he was in Jade's hard body, he wasn't really interested in the kind of focus and intensity it would've taken to get her there. He liked his wings. He liked his beer. He liked things light and easy. The last thing he wanted was a running partner—or a lifting partner.

In one fluid motion, Jade wrapped her heavy black hair into a loose bun on the top of her head and secured it with an elastic band. There was nothing comfortable about the way every part of her was ripped, cut, and banging. It gave her a definite advantage.

"Hey," she said all calm, cool, and collected. "Are you ready for this?"

"Not exactly." He dropped his duffle bag on a nearby bench and shoved his hands in his sweatpants pockets. "Where's Amelia?"

"Checking on something electrical in Pop's office."

"Who's Pop?"

"My friend Tanya's dad. He owns this place. His son runs it now, but we still call it Pop's office."

So, this was Jade's turf, and weight lifting was Jade's sport. Did he get any kind of advantage?

Amelia walked out of a nearby room. "Rome, nice you see you made it."

"Like I had a choice."

"You always have a choice."

Yeah, if unemployment was a choice. "How's this going to work?"

Amelia pointed to the far wall. "We're set up over there. Normal show until the second hour when Jade's segment is announced and she challenges you to a lift off. The cameras will be rolling the whole time and posted online later in the week."

"This is radio," he reminded her.

"But what if it could be more?" Amelia asked cryptically.

He didn't want more, and he was about to say as much when Jade grinned and their eyes met.

"Don't you want the cameras rolling when you beat me? Seeing is believing."

He held her gaze, thinking she was beautiful and feisty enough to make looking like a fool on camera seem tempting.

"Good point," he said. "What are we going to be doing? Presses? Squats?"

"Dead lifts," she said, but then she laughed. "I'm kidding. I wouldn't want to hurt you."

He narrowed his eyes in challenge. "Dead lifts it is."

Amelia clapped. "Excellent."

"No!" Jade walked toward him and lowered her voice. "You'll kill your lower back if you don't know what you're doing."

His pride stepped up to handle this. "What makes you think I don't know what I'm doing?"

She made a face. "Call it a hunch."

"We're going in fifteen!" Amelia yelled.

"Excellent!" Rome yelled back. He was a sitting duck, and he just wanted to get it over with.

With one hand on his collar at the back of his neck, he whipped his sweatshirt over his head, accidentally taking his T-shirt along with it.

Jade's eyes widened briefly as she scanned his bare torso.

Maybe he wasn't at a complete disadvantage after all.

He tossed his sweatshirt *and* his T-shirt aside and then headed for the table.

"You're going to do the show shirtless?"

He could hear her moving behind him.

"Yep."

"Why? Because there are cameras?"

He stopped, turned, and she ran right into him. Instant heat. With his hands around her elbows, and her bare belly pressed against his, he couldn't help but smile. "I don't care about the cameras. I just figured if you can do the show dressed like that, then I can do the show dressed like this." She looked down quickly, and when she looked back up, her cheeks were pink. "I'm striving for inclusion and equality now, if you haven't heard" he said. "And, this is about as equal as I can get—unless you have another pair of hot pants in your locker I can borrow."

She laughed, her chest rising and falling between them, and he gave her arms a little squeeze before they parted ways.

When he reached the table, Amelia rolled her eyes. "Put on your shirt."

He put on his headset instead.

"In five, four, three, two ..." Amelia's voice was replaced by the guitar riff lead-in to the *Riled Up with Rome* voiceover, and then, it was show time.

"How ya doin', folks? Thanks for joining me. I'm Rome Rizzelli, coming to you live from Pop's Gym & Ring in South City, where you're in for a real treat, and I'm in for ..." he glanced at the beauty sitting next to him, "God only knows."

Jade was smiling from ear to ear.

He spent the first hour running through his notes from that morning. The Indians' latest injuries and ever-darkening playoff hopes. The Cavs record-breaking, multiyear, free-agent signing.

And more drama than a daytime soap opera in the Boltz front office. Jade waited patiently and unflinchingly for her turn on the mic. He was about to give her a stellar introduction when Amelia broke in with some hokey voiceover and swelling orchestra music that announced Man vs. Woman, complete with an annoying echo and the tagline: *We're Keeping Score.*

He adjusted his headset and thought to flash his middle finger in Amelia's direction when a cameraman dropped to one knee in front of the broadcast table. This entire setup was ludicrous.

"The things you'll do for a paycheck," he said, glancing at Jade, who had leaned closer to her laptop screen, looking sexy as hell barely dressed and clearly concentrating. "Let me introduce you to Jade Wren. You may remember her as a past guest and caller. Chances are, she's left an impression. She's sure left an impression on me."

She gave him the slightest sideways glance, and her lips twitched.

"Welcome—again—to *Riled Up with Rome*, Jade."

"Thank you," she said. "I'm excited to be here for the very first Man vs. Woman."

He snorted. "I'm glad somebody is."

"Are you afraid?" She tossed him a full-blown smile that stoked his already humming libido.

"Nope." But the more reasonable, off-air part of him bristled the smallest bit. The only comfort was knowing if she lifted more than him, at least he'd get to watch her do it.

"Okay, so here's the deal. Because you clearly think your penis makes you all-powerful ..."

He coughed a laugh. "I never said that."

"Maybe not in so many words, but you've insinuated more than once that men are stronger and faster and, therefore, the better and more entertaining athletes."

"I never insinuated that. I said that loud and clear, because ..." he reached beyond his laptop for the air horn, "that's the truth, and if you don't like it you can ..."

"Yeah, yeah, yeah. We know how it goes. So save it. Now, it's time for you to put your money where your mouth is." Big grin. Eyes sparkling.

Clearly, she was enjoying this, and that had him off his game again, giving her even more of an upper hand while he suddenly thought of something else he'd like to put where his mouth was.

"I have a challenge for you," she said.

"What'd you have in mind?" he asked, playing along. "Dead lifts?"

She rolled her eyes. "Not unless you have a death wish. I was thinking more along the lines of regular old bench presses. Can you bench-press, Rome?"

"Yes, I can bench-press."

"When was the last time you bench-pressed?"

"Honestly? College. But it's like riding a bike, right?"

She laughed. "Sure it is. What was your personal best in college?"

"I have no idea."

"Long time ago, huh?"

"Ha ha. I'm thirty-one. That's hardly old. And folks, you should know that Jade is a hobby bodybuilder, so she clearly thinks she's got this in the bag."

"If men are the stronger gender, like you so readily claim, then I couldn't possibly have it in the bag. Why don't we see who comes out on top?"

Oh, all this back and forth had him pretty clear about who he'd like to see on top. "Ladies first."

By now, they had an audience. He recognized the woman with blue-tipped hair and an armful of tattoos as one of Jade's teammates. And when Jade left the table and sauntered across the gym like it was a runway, complete with a cameraman trailing behind, it was clear by the noise level in the gym that she was the crowd favorite.

"This could be rigged, folks. I want a thorough check of those weights before she uses them." He leaned back in his chair and watched her sprawl out on the bench.

He had the best seat in the house. "From here it looks like Jade is set to bench ..." he squinted to make sure he was right, "105 pounds." He hid a smirk behind his hand, because he could bench that. No problem.

But then she benched 105—eight reps to be exact—with no problem, too. She slipped off the bench while the lunkheads beside her set up another lift. *Warm-up sets.* She was just getting started.

He kept chatting away, took a couple callers, both of whom declared votes for him as if they had an official poll running. Just in case, Rome snagged a pencil from the table and scratched down two hash marks beneath his name.

"The next lift looks set for ..." Rome squinted again, "130 pounds."

He could bench that, too. Hell, he could bench his weight, which was 185. Well, at least he used to bench his weight and then some back in college.

Jade did five reps with ease.

One hundred and thirty pounds led to 145 pounds, which led to one rep at 165 pounds. That was her weight according to the team roster. Surely, she was done there, and he had an excellent shot of beating her. But then ... the lunks set her up for 175 pounds, a little too close to his weight for comfort.

She slipped back onto the bench and adjusted her grip. The muscles in her legs flexed as she lowered the bar to her chest, and then with a throaty sound that had his balls tightening, she raised that son-of-a-bitch five times—two more times than they'd agreed upon for qualifying's sake. Did that mean he had to lift the same weight six times to beat her? *Shit.*

Rome swiped at the beads of sweat on his forehead and tried to look nonplussed as she made her way back to him, swinging those hips and dragging a towel over her glistening skin.

"Looks like I'm up, folks." In more ways than one, because that was just how jacked this day was. "Stay tuned, because after the break, I'm going to show Ms. Wren how it's done." He pulled off his headset, discreetly adjusted his randy half under the table, and headed for the bench.

"Good luck," she called out real pretty-like as she passed.

He turned around until he was walking backward, so he could throw her some shade, but when he did, he saw she'd turned too, and unless he was mistaken, she was totally checking him out.

Of course she was checking him out. She was the one who'd kissed him.

With a fresh surge of confidence, he smiled and raised his arms to his sides. "Get a good look, sweetheart. Maybe later, I'll let you touch."

Chapter Seven

Jade smoothed her hand over Rome's shoulder to his chest, pressing lightly. "Here?"

He grimaced. "Yep."

Four reps into his 175-pound bench press, he'd cried out like a sick animal and lost his grip on the bar. She knew enough about anatomy and had seen too many lifting injuries not to know he'd torn something, but he'd played it off like he'd just given out because he was tired and then pissed because Jade had won. She hadn't missed the winces, though, as he'd made his way back to the table and gruffly finished the radio show.

Once Amelia and the crew had cleaned up their equipment and moved out, and Jillian and Tanya had climbed into the ring for their afternoon sparring session, Jade backed Rome into a literal and figurative corner.

"I'm telling you, you tore your pec." The question was, how severe was the tear? She walked her fingertips to his armpit, pushing here and there. Her good friend MJ Rooney's husband, Tag, was a sports medicine doctor. Maybe he could fit Rome in for an exam.

"I told you I'd let you touch me."

She glanced up, and he was smiling. In the drama and worry of it all, she'd forgotten about the silly quip. Her hand stalled over his heart, and her eyes locked with his. A heat that had nothing to do with weight lifting spread from her face to her chest, to the tingly space between her legs. And she felt like she was back on the steps at Ballers'.

Get a grip. Yes, she was touching him, but it was for a practical reason. But still, she could imagine a few impractical touches that she would like to try. A swipe of his flat abs. A finger walk along his happy trail. How would he kiss her if she touched him like that? More than a brush of his lips. More than a gentle sweep of his tongue. What would it take to really send him off the rails?

Not that she ever intended to really find out.

She cleared her throat. "This is a serious injury, Rome. You should've warmed up."

He nodded. "Well, I know that now—a little too late. I thought I had better control of the situation."

She gave him a sympathetic but superior look. "You need to see a doctor. I can get you in to see the best." She dug into the bag at her feet for her phone.

Tag didn't answer, and she wasn't surprised when she had to leave a message. He was a busy man. They would just have to wait for him to call back. But as she paced while she left the message, she noticed Tanya and Jillian looking at her funny from their perch in the ring. She knew the way they thought, especially Jillian. And after she'd fessed up about the kiss on the steps at Ballers', they probably had reason to be suspicious of this scene.

They were so not waiting in this fish bowl.

"Tag will call back soon," she said to Rome. "In the meantime ..." she glanced at her friends, "We can go to my place. It's only a couple blocks away. We can get you ice, and you'll feel better."

The minute she said it, her chest clenched in panic. She just invited him back to her empty apartment on the heels of some serious flirting. That had to be bad judgment. But right away, her brain scrambled to refute it. The man was injured. She was helping him. That's what a *good girl* did.

"Your shirt." She picked it up off the ground and handed it to him. Covering him up would help her keep some perspective.

He took the shirt in his left hand, grinning all the while like he'd hit the jackpot instead of torn his pec. "I might need help with this."

Since she was being helpful, she obliged, easing the soft cotton that smelled crisp and clean over his head and past the injured part of his body. He didn't do much to assist. He mostly watched her. And she was unbelievably getting turned on by dressing him. Wasn't that backward?

She needed to get out of this gym. Put some distance between them. Get some fresh air into her lungs.

"Where you going?" Tanya called out as they passed.

"Home. We're waiting for Tag to call."

Tanya nodded. "Good luck."

Jillian laughed. "Sure you are," she said under her breath as Jade and Rome moved past the ring.

Damn, Jillian. But she wasn't a psychic. Just because the woman expected something to happen didn't mean it would.

Once Jade reached the apartment, she kept space between her and Rome. She directed him to the couch, handed him a package of frozen peas for his chest, and then hung out in the kitchen, staring at her phone, willing Tag to call so they could be on their merry way.

"I really think I'm fine," Rome said.

She looked at the back of his head, poking up from the couch. "How can you say that? You couldn't even put on your shirt."

"Well, I never said I couldn't do it. I just said I needed help." He glanced back at her and smiled.

She charged into the living room and glared at him. "Then go ahead. Show me. Take it off and prove you're fine."

He chuckled. "Are you asking me to take off my shirt?"

She was not going to get sucked into something seedy. "Yes, because I know I'm right. I know you tore your pec."

He dragged the hem of his shirt seductively over his abs, and she looked away.

"Some music would be nice, don't you think?" He attempted to hum some swanky striptease song.

She stifled a laugh and looked at him. "Use your right hand, hot shot. That's the side you hurt."

He paused, and something serious flashed in his eyes before he barreled through, lifting the shirt over his head with his right arm. Unfortunately for him, he couldn't quite coordinate the grimace with the passing of the shirt across his face, and Jade saw every bit of pain.

"Rome!" She dropped to the couch beside him, picking up the package of peas and setting it against his chest. "You're hurt. Admit it."

He rested his head on the back of the sofa and exhaled. "Okay. I admit it. But, it doesn't do me any good. I can't be hurt. I just can't."

"Why?" Maybe she shouldn't have asked. It really was none of her business. But he looked so defeated. "Everybody gets hurt. You'll mend."

He shook his head, and then his eyes roamed her face for the longest time, like he was trying to decide what came next. "My mother isn't the only person I'm responsible for. I have a sister, Tess. She's a little younger than you, but she has Down syndrome. I'm ... I'm just not the one who ever needs to be taken care of."

"Well ..." She struggled to find the right words. "It won't be forever, and there's nothing wrong with needing someone to take care of you every now and then." She lifted the package off his shoulder and touched his skin just to make sure it wasn't too cold. Maybe she should get a dish towel and ...

He grabbed her wrist, and his green eyes darkened as she looked deeply into them. "Maybe one kiss would make it better," he said.

A nervous hole formed in her stomach. "We already had one kiss."

"So you have a quota on kisses like you have a quota on beers?"

"Something like that." But her voice had dropped to almost a whisper and her heart was pounding out of her chest.

"Why?" He slid his hand gently up and down her arm, and she didn't even try to pretend there weren't goose pimples all over her skin.

"Because I'm not interested in anything serious."

He smiled. "Me, neither. I'd say that makes us the perfect fit. A little fun on air and off. Nothing serious."

Well, when he said it like that ...

"Okay. But ..." The rest of the sentence disappeared into his open mouth as he slid his hand from her wrist to the back of her neck and pulled her in.

Oh. My. God. This was nothing like the kiss on the steps. This was hot, hard, and so damn needy she couldn't catch her breath. It was nothing like any kiss in her recent memory. But to be fair, there weren't many of them. She could count the number of men who had seen the inside of this apartment by her invitation on one hand.

Rome's tongue darted in and out of her mouth, and she matched his eager pace, fully aware that she didn't get to voice her concerns about what this would mean for working together. But if they were both on the same page, if neither one of them wanted anything serious, then what was the big deal?

She would be gone from WKST before it ever had a chance to become an issue.

There. Decision made. For better or for worse. On impulse, she straddled him, braced her hands against the seatback on either side of his head, and well and truly had her way with his mouth. She might've worried about his injury if she didn't already feel his erection burning a hole in her spandex.

He surprised the heck out of her when he simultaneously tugged on the front of her sports bra and freed a breast. He tugged again, and the other released. Then, he leaned forward and licked a path from the base of her neck to the depths of her cleavage, making her shudder. *Damn.* Her nipples were hard by the time he licked lazy circles around them.

She tried not to think about how easy she was making this. *Good girls* weren't easy, but they were allowed to have fun, too. And this, this was ... *Mmm.*

In a matter of seconds, she was completely naked and helping him out of his sweatpants.

Thank God for Jillian, because the wild woman had condoms stashed around this place like they were Tic Tacs. Jade grabbed one from the coffee table drawer, rolled it on, and then kissed a path up his body from belly to neck before she rubbed against his length and kissed his mouth. Sex could be therapeutic, couldn't it? Maybe the endorphins would make his injury feel better. *Still trying to be helpful,* she thought sarcastically.

And then she slid onto him. Softly. Gently. Until he filled her to the point of devilish ache. "I'll go slow," she said. "So we don't hurt your pec."

His easy laugh rumbled through her. "Hurt the pec. Slow will kill me."

Once, twice, she tested that theory. Then, she lifted and settled again, watching the power of her movement sweep across his face, tightening his muscles until he closed his eyes.

A rough sound vibrated in his throat as he pushed into her. Then, his fingers found her center, touching, teasing, until she was riding him faster without conscious thought.

Carried away. So far gone she almost didn't hear her phone ring.

• • •

Rome struggled to pull up his sweatpants with one hand, after Jade ran off naked to take a call from her doctor friend. When he'd finally successfully dragged the elastic band over his ass and settled his back to the couch again, he felt like he'd run a marathon. How was he going to take care of his mother like this? She hated that wheelchair. Said it made her feel like an invalid. Reminded Rome that for the year his father had been alive after her accident, he'd carried her from the bed to the chair every morning and night. And that's exactly what Rome did. Until now. He dropped his head to the back of the couch and closed his eyes, the thick warmth of a recent orgasm settling him and no doubt skewing the magnitude of all of this. Man, they'd really gone and gotten carried away here.

"I'll bring him in. Thank you." Jade's voice grew louder.

By the time Rome lifted his head and opened his eyes, she was standing in front of him, wrapped in a silky yellow robe that stopped above her knees. The gym clothes she'd been wearing were scattered on the floor at her feet. And the sight of her was breathtaking.

"Tag can fit you in today. After four but before six. When should we go?"

Shit. It was Wednesday, Tess needed a ride to the grocery store where she worked as a bagger. And her five o'clock shift put that ride smack in the middle of Jade's time range. Maybe he could ask Aunt Karen to stay a little longer tonight and give Tess a ride to the store on her way home. But he hated to do that. His mother and sister were his responsibility. Besides, he didn't want to drag Jade into the mix. "We shouldn't. I'll be fine."

"You *have* to see a doctor," Jade said, obviously perturbed.

"I know!" He didn't mean to snap. He wasn't even sure that two simple words spoken with an ounce of force qualified as snapping, but the look on Jade's face told him she thought they did. "I just can't get there today."

She tightened her robe around her throat, and with a lift of her chin and a cock of her head, she said, "I'm just trying to help you."

A *click-clack* then a *creak* drew their attention to the front door, where the chick with tattoos and blue hair appeared, smiling.

"I gave you just enough time, didn't I? Sorry to barge in. Well, sorry not sorry, because I need to grab something from my room. I'll be gone in a flash." She strolled by the couch and eyed them up. "I always did like that robe on you, sexy thang."

Jade didn't look like she appreciated the compliment in the heat of the moment. "That's my roommate, Jillian."

"Nice to meet you, Jillian," Rome called to the shadow down the hall, but then he locked his eyes on Jade and held her gaze. "I should go."

"How are you going to do that? You can't drive a stick with a tear."

"I'll be fine. I promise." And to prove it, he stood up and snatched his shirt off the floor with his right hand, swallowing the scream that rose in his throat when it felt like he ripped the son-of-a-bitch all over again.

"Good luck with that."

She could've frozen Lake Erie with those eyes, but she would've thawed it a second later when the thin robe fell open over a good chunk of breast.

He walked to her. "Thank you."

"For what? I didn't do anything. You won't let me do anything." She stepped back.

He reached for her with his good arm and pulled until she walked the rest of the way to him. "Thank you for your concern," he said.

Her cold eyes heated and her voice thickened with something that almost sounded like seduction. "I'm not concerned."

He chuckled. "Then I appreciate your enthusiasm." He grabbed a fistful of robe until he felt the flesh of her ass and nuzzled her neck while her leg lifted over his thigh. "Don't worry about me. Nothing serious, remember?"

"Holy shit! I'm still here," the roommate said, laughing.

With one last kiss to the base of Jade's throat, Rome released her. "And I'm gone." He loved how her flushed face and full lips lingered as he backed away.

He sort of had to hand it to Amelia. Torn pec and all, Man vs. Woman had been quite the success.

•••

Jade watched the front door close behind Rome. "He should not be driving. What an ass."

"From what I could see, it does look like a nice ass." Jillian grinned suggestively.

Well, Jade had ridden him like a thoroughbred, so ... "I can't speak for his ass. I didn't get to see it. The rest of him isn't bad, though—for a little fun on the side." Something she knew Jillian would totally understand. Her mother and grandmother on the other hand ... Jade felt the beginnings of a dry heave.

Rome Rizzelli was not the kind of guy she could ever bring home. The mere fact he was an American she'd met in a bar would remind them too much of her dad. Not that she would ever have a reason to bring him home or even introduce them for that matter. Temporary. Fun. That was all that was happening here.

Jade eyed the wad of black leather clothing Jillian had tossed over her shoulder and decided to change the topic. "Get what you came for?"

Jillian cracked open a soda can and nodded. "Riding gear. I'm trying to convince Carter to get us matching Harleys so we can take a July Fourth road trip."

"In the middle of playoffs? That's a bad idea. What if you get hurt?"

"You sound like Carter. I'll tell you the same thing I told him. That's why they make helmets, and on a motorcycle, at least, I promise to drive *closer* to the speed limit. Fun in the right dose never hurt anybody."

Speaking of people getting hurt ... "Shoot. I need to call Tag back and tell him not to wait around for Rome." She reached for her phone just in time for it to ring. The numbers weren't familiar. "Who's that?"

"How should I know?" Jillian asked. "Answer it."

Jade faced all unknown callers with trepidation—somewhere in the back of her mind, she always thought it would be her dad, resurfacing to cause more grief—but the compulsion to answer this one was strong. Maybe it was Rome, realizing the error of his ways.

Ha. Sure. She'd let it go to voice mail.

"Maybe it's about a job," Jillian added.

That would be excellent. Then she would have direction for this fall.

"Unless ..." Jillian continued, "you would rather stay at the station. From what I saw at Ballers' two weeks ago and then again today, you're damn good at it."

Jade grinned. "Thanks for saying that."

"It wasn't a charity compliment, woman. I'm serious. So serious, I say you give it a few weeks, and then you walk in there and ask to be hired full time." Jillian said. "That producer seems like she would be game."

Maybe. But the idea of doing it seemed outrageous. Sure, Jade liked waking up and pouring over the latest sports headlines, and being on air was a rush. Giving women sports fans a voice in a male-dominated world was even better. But turning to radio as a full-time gig?

"I'm a teacher," she said. "I want a salary, benefits, summers off, and a pension." Funny, when she said those things, they echoed in her head as a chorus of her mother and grandmother's voices.

"Well then, hopefully that call's about a teaching job."

Exactly.

When the ringing stopped, the screen returned to its normal icon-riddled state. "We'll see if they leave a message."

They did.

"Jade, my name is Lois Comella. I'm calling from the Cleveland Metropolitan School District. Your résumé came through our online Human Resources Portal, and we'd like to invite you in after the holiday for an interview."

"I got an interview with the Cleveland schools."

"Good for you."

It was. Umma and Halmoni would be ecstatic.

So why wasn't she?

Chapter Eight

"How's your friend's pec?"

Jade slapped a serving of red, white, and blue fruit salad on her plate and glanced at Tag. "I don't know. I haven't talked to him in a few days." But she'd thought of him. More than she cared to admit.

"You should call him," Jillian said, grinning. "Maybe he's lonely." Then she snatched up a hotdog and bun and brought MJ into the conversation. "You wouldn't mind another mouth to feed would you?"

MJ stirred the baked beans. "Well, I guess the benefit of that would be his mouth would be full, so he couldn't say something stupid and get his ass kicked."

"I told you guys, he's not really like that. It's his radio personality." Which spilled into his everyday personality now and then. Just like when her phone call with her mother had spilled into her night out at the bar and that kiss.

"I don't get that," Tanya said. "A person should be who a person is 100 percent of the time."

In a perfect world, sure.

"Oh, I get it!" Jillian nodded. "You do what you have to do. Like when I covered up the tats and took Carter to my nephew's christening. I mean, after everything that happened, I really shouldn't have bothered, but it seemed like the best I could do at the time."

"Exactly," Jade said, balancing a full plate along with a bottle of beer, thinking more about how she was hiding a big part of herself from Umma and Halmoni than Rome's health issues now.

Tag lifted a beer out of the ice bucket. "Well, I don't care about the guy's multiple personality disorder. " He chuckled. "I care about his pectoral injury. So seriously, if you want to bring him by tonight, you know where I'll be."

She wasn't surprised by the offer. Tag ran a free clinic in Pop's Gym. Generous didn't begin to describe him. But inviting Rome over to MJ and Tag's July Fourth picnic seemed like a stretch. Everyone else who was here—Tanya and Cam, Jillian and Carter—were couples. And she didn't want to insinuate anything. They had fun. They might have fun again. But they were definitely not headed for anything serious like these people.

She flashed them all a smile and then headed back to the picnic table, which was outfitted in a stars and stripes motif. As she ate, she glanced at her phone a few times. Maybe it wouldn't hurt to text him and make sure he was okay. Still, she fought the suggestion. She cleared her plate, finished her beer, and chatted with her friends until her phone buzzed against the wooden table and grabbed her attention again.

Rome: You were right. I should've seen your friend.

Speak of the devil, and funny how that worked. She grinned and typed back:

Would you mind calling me and saying those words? I don't believe this is really you. Rome Rizzelli only speaks the truth, and he's supposedly never wrong. Except ... Do you remember Jay McAllister?

When she chuckled, Tanya eyed her curiously. "I'm assuming that's not a text from your mother."

"Rome," she said without looking up, because his reply came in:

You just want me to call so you can hear my voice.

"I'm serious!" Jillian nudged her with an elbow. "Invite him over."

She hesitated and then looked at Tag. "Maybe you could just talk to him on the phone."

"Sure. Whatever works for you."

> Jade: Actually, I want you to call me so you can talk to Tag.
> Rome: Just give me his office number, and I'll make an appointment. I'm not going to bother the guy on a holiday.
> Jade: It's not a bother. He actually said he'd take a look at it if you wanted to come over here.

She stared at the words after she hit send. Surely he wouldn't take her up on that if he wouldn't even talk to Tag on the phone.

> Rome: Don't worry about it.

Exactly the kind of answer she'd expected. But as she set down her phone, she wondered if the real reason he'd turned down medical care after sucking it up and texting her about it in the first place wasn't because he was in too much pain to get here.

> Jade: It hurts to drive doesn't it? That's why you won't come.
> Rome: Maybe.
> Jade: What if I come get you?

She didn't send it. She deleted the message and started again, only to type the same thing. Why was she even offering? Because she was being helpful, and she wanted the satisfaction of having Tag back up her initial diagnosis. She liked proving Rome wrong. But come on! It was a holiday, too. It wouldn't hurt to have a little fun.

Rome: You really like watching me eat crow, don't you?
Jade: Ha ha! Absolutely. What's your address?

Twenty minutes later, Jade walked up to an unassuming ranch house at the end of a cul-de-sac. American flags on skinny wooden sticks lined the walkway, and a grapevine wreath wrapped in red, white, and blue star garland hung on the door. It felt strange being here, like once again she'd taken things too far. But she knocked and waited semipatiently.

Rome answered the wooden door and smiled at her through the screen. "There's a catch."

She raised a brow. "What catch?"

"Well, if you want to drag me off to your friend just so you can say I told you so, you have to do something for me first."

Why did her mind immediately think it was something dirty? "Like what?"

"I need to buy my sister some fireworks for later tonight. There's a place about a mile from here. Will you take me?"

"I want to go, too." A short, smiley woman appeared at Rome's side.

"This is my sister, Tess," Rome said.

Jade had already known she had Down syndrome. But seeing her standing by Rome, looking up at him so hopefully, the full weight of what he'd told her on the couch sank in.

Jade smiled. "Hi, Tess. It's nice to meet you."

"Nice to meet you, too. Can I go?" When Tess smiled, her face was nothing but cheeks and teeth. It made Jade think only the hardest heart wouldn't give in.

"Well ..." Rome seemed to think about it. "That might be a little more than Jade bargained for. You take a long time picking out fireworks, kiddo, and we only have minutes this time. But I know what you like. I won't let you down." Rome wrapped an arm around her shoulder and pulled her into a side hug. "I promise."

Tess frowned even as she hugged him back. "Okay."

"I don't mind," Jade blurted.

Rome looked surprised but thankful.

As they piled into Jade's Toyota, Rome teased her. "This is totally a teacher's car."

"Is there something wrong with that?"

"Nope. Not for you, but for me, I prefer something sleeker and faster."

"But your car is old," Tess said.

Jade chuckled.

"Hey, no wisecracks from the peanut gallery. A Porsche doesn't get old. It becomes a classic."

"It sounds like a tank," Tess said.

Jade laughed.

"You're right," Rome said.

It was a little surprising how easy he conceded to Tess, who added that she, "liked the minivan better."

Rome looked back at her and smiled. "I'm glad you like it, kiddo."

Jade glanced at him. He seemed so gentle and easy with his sister, almost fatherly. And that bit about the van. He acted like it was something he had given her. Of course it was. He'd said he was responsible for them. She glanced at him again, and then at Tess's smiling reflection in the rearview mirror.

Tess noticed Jade's curiosity and leaned a little closer to the front seat. "What? Did you want to ask me something about Down syndrome? Rome says that's the best thing to say when people stare."

"Oh. No." Jade felt like such a fool. "I was just wondering what kind of fireworks you like?"

"Big ones," Tess said, seemingly unfazed by any of this. "Green ones. I have to plug my ears when Rome lights them. They whoosh out of the pipe and ..." She laughed. "Last year, the pipe fell over, and the firework went sideways."

Jade looked at him. "That sounds dangerous."

"It was," he said, but then he laughed along with Tess. "What? Nobody got hurt."

"They might this year, considering your handicap."

"Rome's not handicapped, but our mother is," Tess said.

Boy, she was just batting a thousand. "I didn't mean it that way. It was ... it was supposed to be funny, but it wasn't. I'm sorry. I shouldn't have said it."

"I hurt my shoulder, Tess," Rome said, taking some of the heat off Jade. He smiled at her and then looked at his sister in the backseat. "That's why Jade is driving to the gas station, and then she's taking me to see a friend of hers who is a doctor, so I can be back to light the sky on fire."

Jade liked this side of him, but even so, her face wrinkled. "I don't think it's a good idea for you to be lighting off mortar-sized rockets when you've got a torn muscle."

"I'll be fine." He studied her carefully, and then again, he gave a quick glance into the back seat. A bit of concern flashed across his face. "But, if you don't believe me, you're welcome to come help."

"That's a great idea!" Tess said enthusiastically. "Come see the fireworks at our house. They're the best fireworks ever."

Hmm. How did you say no to an invitation like that? How did you say yes? "Maybe."

Tess's toothy grin made it seem as though Jade's decision had been made. Rome looked surprised.

"What?" she asked. "I like fireworks almost as much as I like watching you eat crow."

• • •

The doctor listened attentively while Rome explained the circumstances surrounding his injury. There was a lot of head nodding and noises of affirmation. Then the guy, who was apparently married to the Clash's quarterback, poked and prodded Rome's pec.

Jade already looked vindicated, sitting across from them at the picnic table, wearing wide eyes and a smirk while she stroked the shiny black fur of a Lab mix.

The doc stepped away from Rome and reached into an ice bucket, handing him a bottle of beer. "You need an MRI."

"Okay," Rome said.

Tag cracked open a beer, too.

"Wait!" Jade pressed her palms to the table and raised up a bit. "That's it? I thought you invited him over here to diagnosis a pec tear."

"He needs an MRI. I mean, it definitely sounds like it."

"But it might not be?" Rome asked, eyeing up Jade with a smile.

She looked at Tag and rolled her eyes. "Please. You know it's a tear. I know it's a tear. The dog knows it's a tear."

"It probably is," Tag said. "But let's get the MRI before we start talking absolutes. I'll text my office manager tomorrow and see if we can't get that set in motion."

"Who's in motion?" MJ walked toward the table with a pie in each hand.

She was an attractive woman, tall, fit, but not nearly as fit as Jade. And apparently she liked dessert.

"Careful with those," Tag said smiling.

Rome waited for someone to call the guy out for saying something sexist. But no one did. They let him get away with it, and he wasn't even on air. Where was the uproar proclaiming that if the guy was so worried about the pies, he should get off his ass and help her? God knew if he'd said something like that, people would be all over him.

"Yes, dear," MJ said. "I know how long it took you to bake these."

Rome chuckled at what he assumed to be sarcasm. No doubt, either she baked them or her husband bought them.

Tag smiled at her. "With hands as sure as yours, baby, you're the only person I trust to carry them."

"Hey!" Jillian ran up behind MJ with a gallon of ice cream and a can of whipped cream in her hands. "I'm the receiver. What about me?"

"Honey, we aren't talking about catching the pies."

"Sorry, Jill," Tag said. "I just don't trust you with my pies."

So Tag really did make them?

Rome watched the couple share a quick kiss when MJ's hands were free, then when no utensils were found, Tag ran off into the house to get some.

He didn't know what to make of it. It was all just a little too soft for him, too foreign. He hadn't spent much time watching couples interact since his father had died. And honestly—he glanced at Jade—it made him a little uncomfortable being here.

Across the yard, NFL receiver Cam Simmons and his girlfriend Tanya Martin, who Rome had seen a couple times before, helped Jillian's fiancé, a Clash coach, set up some yard games. Rome wasn't usually the shrinking violet, especially not around athletes, but today, he felt really out of place.

He glanced at Jade, again, who was ripping a label off her bottle of beer. Was she annoyed that Tag hadn't boldly and completely backed her up? Or was she just as uncomfortable as he was. Do the math. Two by two by two by two. Except they weren't a pair.

"Do you play corn hole?" MJ asked him.

"Well, that depends on which kind of corn hole we're talking about."

She looked annoyed. "I only know one kind of corn hole. Bean bag toss."

"He has a torn pec," Jade said.

"He has two arms," MJ countered. "If you can toss with your left, then we'll have even teams."

He laughed. "So that's really why I'm here? To even up the sides."

"You didn't think I wanted you here for your shiny personality, did you?" MJ noticed her husband cutting across the yard, and she ran off to meet him with the dog sprinting along beside her.

"Tough crowd," he said to Jade. But they weren't really. For the most part, they'd been more than welcoming.

"She's a big advocate for antibullying programs in the city."

He nodded slowly. "And she thinks I'm a bully."

"She only knows you on the air. She'll see another side of you today."

If he stayed that long. He wasn't sure he should care enough to show MJ anything. But as he watched the sun filter through the trees and cast dancing shadows on Jade's pretty face, he figured he owed her and her friends quite a bit for letting him and his bum arm crash their holiday. Besides, Jade had saved his ass with Tess today.

"Thanks again for all of this, especially for the fireworks run."

"Of course." But there was more in the way she studied him, a curiosity that made him feel uncomfortable and look away. "What happened to your mom? Why is she handicapped?"

Rome took a pull of his beer and then another before returning the bottle to the table. "She used to work for the electric company. She wasn't wearing a harness like she was supposed to while using the lift. Somehow she put the thing in motion without knowing, and she hit her head on a roof overhang, which knocked her out and caused her to fall twenty feet."

"Oh my God! That's awful. Is she paralyzed?"

He shook his head. "No, but she thinks she should be." At Jade's surprised look, he added. "Don't get me wrong. The nerve damage was bad, and on top of that, she had multiple surgeries to fix a shattered pelvis and fractures in her legs, but fifteen years later, her reality doesn't match up with what the doctors find when they run tests. I think it's mental," he added, even though he didn't tell many people that. "That frustrates the hell out of me. I always hoped she'd get better. At least for Tess's sake."

He knew he'd said too much the minute he noted the pity in her eyes. Sometimes it really was easier being loudmouthed, "who cares" Rome Rizzelli, because nobody ever looked at that guy like Jade was right now.

"Maybe I'll just fix her good and send her off to a nursing home," he added.

So much for the pity. Jade looked shocked, now, and a little wary. He tried to tell himself that was better than the pity.

"I don't believe you," she said suddenly. "When we were buying fireworks, Tess told me you light them off every year just like your dad used to do. She also told me she doesn't remember a lot about when your dad used to do it, but your mom does, and when you do it, it makes her smile. That doesn't sound like the kind of hard ass who would lock his mother away in a nursing home."

He shrugged, his mouth softening a bit. "I guess it depends on the day."

"Pie first, games later," Tag called from the middle of the yard, summoning everyone to the table.

"We'll play one game," Jade said. "Then I'm taking you home and helping you get set up for fireworks."

"You don't have to do that. Really. I was kidding when I invited you." Mostly.

"Well, I want to do it. Besides, I already told Tess I would. I don't want to disappoint her."

And that, at least, made two of them.

Chapter Nine

"So you're coworkers, huh?" Rome's mother, Bea, gave Jade the once over now that Jade was standing in her living room.

The woman was short, frail, and covered in alligator-like skin. Her blond hair was cropped, and her clothes were two sizes too big. She looked rough, but she had Rome's sharp green eyes and a hint of his charming smile.

"Are you Chinese?" she asked.

Jade shook her head. "My mother is from Korea. My father is American."

"You're a very pretty girl."

"Thank you."

"Don't go drawing any conclusions, Mom," Rome said. "We work together. That's it. And I didn't invite her here to be grilled. I invited her here for the fireworks."

To help with the fireworks, she corrected him in her head. And the guy needed help with a lot more than that. She didn't know how he managed to keep everything together around here with two hands, let alone one that was now in a sling thanks to Tag's home medical supply stash.

Bea's thinning brows rose. "The fireworks aren't *that* good."

Ha! Rome came by his sharp tongue honestly, and Jade didn't blame the woman for being suspicious.

"They'll probably be worse with you wearing that thing," Bea said.

Rome looked down at the sling. "I'm not worried."

But Jade was.

"What'd the doctor say?" Bea asked.

"I need an MRI."

"Did he prescribe pain meds?" his mother asked.

Darkness slashed across Rome's face, and the temperature in the room dropped a good twenty degrees. "No. I'm not in that much pain. And even if I was, I wouldn't take that shit. It's a death sentence."

He stared hard at his mother, and Jade's discomfort grew. But instead of a colossal confrontation like Jade expected, Rome's mother turned her head and looked out the window. "Leave me in here this year. You can't carry me out with your arm like that anyway."

He carried her? Everywhere? Why? If she couldn't walk, why didn't she use a wheelchair?

Bea crossed her legs at the ankles, and the easy motion didn't get past Jade. She thought back to the conversation at MJ's house. *I think it's mental*, he'd said. Maybe carrying her around now and then was easier than arguing with her 24-7. It was just another example of how off-air Rome was different. She couldn't even imagine how on-air Rome would handle this.

"You're coming out, and that's final," he said to his mother.

Well, maybe he would handle it like that. No conversation. Just an "I'm right and you're wrong" command. But as rough as he'd sounded, a softness lingered in his eyes. "I don't want you to miss this. I'll get your wheelchair."

Bea snorted and waved him off. "You can't even lift me into my wheelchair."

What a harsh woman! Jade wished there was something she could say to make the woman realize how lucky she was to have a son who would even put up with this. And then there was Tess, who rifled through the bags of fireworks over and over again without a care in the world, like all this bickering was normal.

"Mom, you can walk," Rome said. "You're not paralyzed." He started down the hall in a huff. "Aunt Karen said you walk for her all the time."

Jade sat there, feeling very uncomfortable and thinking she shouldn't have come. She should've dropped him off and gone back to MJ's, where she would be sipping mojitos under the stars and watching fireworks with her friends ... while Rome was back here dealing with all of this. But that bothered her. A lot.

Bea looked at Jade. "I worked for the electric company for twenty years until their crap equipment tossed me from a bucket ladder. I've been in pain ever since."

It wasn't quite the story she'd gotten from Rome, but either way, it was sad. "I'm sorry."

"He expects too much from me."

Maybe. Rome could be loud and opinionated—even when the opinion wasn't popular—but Jade had also seen another side of him, the side that stepped up to run this house.

"I'm sure he just wants the best for you," Jade said with a smile, and then she asked Tess, who was still rifling through the bags, if she needed help finding something.

"No. I just like looking at them," Tess said. "This one and this one are my favorites." She held up two fat cylinders with flowers on the labels.

"Her father used to light off the fireworks every year, so Rome took over after he died."

"I know. He told me."

Bea really eyed her up then. Jade tried not to squirm. It wasn't like it had been pillow talk or anything incredibly intimate and moving. They weren't like that. It was information, plain and simple, between two people who happened to have a lusty attraction that led to random kisses and sofa sex. That sort of thing didn't have any true staying power, so Bea had nothing to worry about. Jade wasn't trying to horn in. Just help. Because he certainly didn't seem to have enough of it.

"Tess, you wanna help me get her in the chair and wheel her out?" Rome pushed the wheelchair with his good arm.

"I'll do it," Jade said automatically. "That way Tess can keep an eye on the fireworks."

Tess smiled, and Rome didn't argue. In fact, he looked relieved.

She'd done the right thing coming here tonight. Even if a little part of her had started questioning exactly what was happening.

...

Rome watched Jade carry twenty-eight-pound cinder blocks into the yard, so he could set the fireworks inside of them like his father had always done. Talk about a role reversal. He was sort of helpless here, and he wasn't used to it. Not one bit. But what could he do? As much as he hadn't wanted to draw her into the middle of his family dynamics, he needed her help.

"Where do you want it?" she asked.

Rome walked to the dead center of the yard and tapped his foot on the ground. "My dad always put one here." And then, he walked backward fifty steps. "He put another one here. That way, they're far enough from the house and the garage to keep everything and everyone safe."

Jade squatted to drop the block. She was all muscular precision, protecting her back with the strength of her tanned legs that went on for miles and miles in a pair of little white shorts. And don't even get him started on her arms. Who knew triceps could be the sexiest part of a woman's body?

"What was your dad like?" she asked as she straightened.

The question took him off guard, and he looked up at the waning sun. It had been a long time since he'd talked about his dad in anything more than passing. He wasn't really sure he wanted to do it now. This thing was supposed to be fun, not serious.

"My dad was an awful man," she said, surprising him. "He never would've done something like this for me. So, I'm assuming your dad was something special."

He had been, but that word "awful" sort of stuck with Rome, and it didn't feel right to gloss over that in favor of talking up his dad. "Why was your father so awful?"

"He was an alcoholic who liked to hit us. Well, he mostly hit my mother and then threatened to hit her more if my grandmother or I intervened. Then he left when I was nine. That was actually the nicest thing he ever did." She didn't look sad. She didn't look angry. She just said the words like they were a matter of fact rather than a noose around her neck.

He couldn't help but admire that. In fact, he wished he could be more like that with some of the stuff that happened around here.

"What a fucking loser," Rome said.

She nodded. "Well, if you ask my mother and grandmother, apparently the world is full of them. And it's their job to keep me from those clutches."

Which made him think about her hang-up with "horrible American" men. Now it made perfect sense.

"My dad wasn't one of them. He was goofy, and dependable, and the biggest football fan you've ever seen. He painted his face on game day just to sit in his recliner at home."

"Seriously?"

Rome nodded. "He used to quiz me on statistics and history. Go ahead. Ask me something about the Boltz. Anything. But make it obscure so I can really impress you."

She laughed. "If I make it too obscure, then I won't know the answer even if it's right, and I won't be impressed."

"True." He smiled at her for the longest time.

"What?"

He probably shouldn't say it, but what the hell. He'd never been one to hold back random thoughts before. "I think my dad would've liked you. He would've been impressed."

She grinned. "Because I can lift more than his son or because I drink beer from a bottle?"

Something weird happened to the air between them. It thinned, making Rome's breathing shallow. That bit his dad had told him about the bottle being proof his mother would be more than a lover ... she would be a friend? Yeah, that. Rome felt it deep in his core. With his life the way it was, he didn't have many lovers or friends. And if that stint on her couch hadn't been some one-off fluke brought on by too much postlifting testosterone and adrenaline, he may have found both—for the short term at least.

"I got the music all ready to go."

It was Tess, scrambling down the yard with exhilaration in every step.

"How much longer?" she asked.

"It's not even dark yet, kiddo." But man, he loved her enthusiasm.

Thirty minutes later, the sun had gone down and setup was complete. Aside from the cinder blocks used to stabilize the fountain fireworks Tess loved so much, the yard was littered with two aerial tubes his father had constructed out of plastic piping and wood more than twenty years ago.

In the moonlight, Rome could see Jade standing beside him holding the mini butane torch his father had taught him to use. "You do know it's illegal to light these off in Ohio," she said.

Rome shrugged off her concern. "My theory has always been if you can buy them here, you can light them here. The fireworks law in this state is backward." He extended his left hand toward her. "Give it to me."

"Why? You can't use a torch with a sling. What if it catches on fire?"

He laughed.

"It's not funny."

"It is." He stepped closer. "You know, for a girl who was gutsy enough to kiss a stranger in a stairwell, you worry about an awful lot of things. What's that all about?" Almost immediately, he started mentally answering his own question. Her comment about kissing him to prove a point. Taking the radio job to push herself.

Sex on her sofa. Illegal fireworks. It was all about taking back something—everything—her father had stolen from her. Wasn't it? He didn't need to hear her say it. He didn't want to see her upset. "You know what? Don't answer that. I think I know."

She tilted her head. "Really? You think you know me that well?"

He hemmed and hawed. "I think I'm getting there."

After a few beats of heavy silence, she stepped back into the shadows. "You're still not getting the torch, Rizzelli."

"There is no way a woman like you wants to risk a criminal record."

"And you do?"

"Sure, why not? It goes along with the image. Besides, this is my family we're talking about. Look." He unhooked the sling from around his neck and let it drop to the ground. "Now, nothing can catch on fire. Okay? You were right there when Tag said I could light off the fireworks, just no heavy lifting."

Slowly, she held out the torch to him. "Fine. But, I'm only conceding because I've never done this before. I'm not really even sure how to light this thing."

"And here I thought you just wanted to see me arrested." He closed his hand around the torch, touching her hand in the process, and he didn't let go even though he could. "Thank you for everything you did today."

"Of course. You needed help, and I could help."

"Was that the only reason?" He pulled on her hand, and she walked closer until their lips were inches apart.

"It's the only reason I care to admit." And then just like she had on the steps at Ballers' bar, she kissed him.

Soft and sweet until they both turned up the heat.

"Rome, where are these damn fireworks?" His mother's voice filtered through the haze.

He smiled against Jade's lips and whispered. "I think they already started."

Chapter Ten

"Hey."

Rome looked up from his laptop screen and smiled at the beautiful woman standing in the doorway to his office. She was wearing a ruffled blouse and a mini skirt.

His Monday morning was starting off all kinds of right.

"Hey, yourself. How was the rest of your weekend?"

"Good. How's your arm?" She gave a pointed look at the area in question.

"It's good. Why the face?"

She stepped closer with her eyes narrowed. "Where's the sling? You're supposed to wear it until you see Tag again."

"I don't need it." She made a face, and he rushed to strengthen his argument. "Seriously. I drove this morning, and it barely hurt."

She shook her head as she rounded his desk and perched on the corner. "That's a pretty miraculous recovery."

Her bare leg brushed his, and he reached out to smooth a hand up her calf to the bend of her knee. "What can I say? I'm tough."

She seemed to think about that before she leaned in, filling the air with her spicy perfume. "You're not that tough, Rome. You couldn't even carry a cement block. When's the MRI? Have you heard from Tag's office yet?"

Part of him wanted to tell her to back off—the part of him that wasn't used to anyone caring. But another part of him had the odd reaction of not wanting to disappoint her.

Yet another part of him badly wanted to slip a hand between her thighs in the middle of a workday.

He started with his fingertips grazing the inside of her knee, but a knock on the door jamb foiled his plan.

Jade jumped back, adjusting her skirt and her guilty expression.

"Come on in," he called through a laugh.

"Oh good. You're both here." Amelia clutched her trusty stainless steel coffee mug in one hand and a stack of bound papers in another. "Our next Man vs. Woman will be Wednesday at Carson High School Field."

Rome groaned. He wasn't as pain-free as he'd claimed to be.

"Think quarterback challenge," Amelia said.

Nope. No way was that happening. "Listen …"

"Could we do something else, like maybe soccer instead?" Jade asked. "I have my conference championship Saturday and serious practices all this week. I could use a break from football." She smiled, but she wasn't fooling him. She was saving his ass, wasn't she? Just like she'd been prepared to save his ass last night with the butane torch.

Amelia gnawed on her lip as she considered it. "Are you any good at soccer?"

Jade nodded. "Very good."

"How about you?" she asked Rome.

"Never played."

"Then soccer it is." She walked out of the office with a spring in her step.

That woman lived to see him fail.

"The good news is you don't need your pecs to kick a soccer ball," Jade said.

No, the good news was he'd had sex with a woman who'd witnessed his crazy family dynamics, and she hadn't run away from him yet. "Close the door and come here," he said.

She shook her head as she backed away with a smile. "We have a show to do."

He looked at the clock. "We have forty minutes."

"I know, but I have to talk to Amelia about something. Sorry." She smiled. "Rain check?"

"You bet your sweet ass."

And if he hadn't been so mesmerized by her curves in that short skirt, he may have thought to ask what she needed to talk to Amelia about.

...

Jade knocked on Amelia's doorjamb.

"Hey, come on in. I was just about to call the athletic director at Carson to see what sort of soccer equipment they have."

"We just need a net and some balls." If they kept it simple, Rome wouldn't get hurt any more than he already was. That tough guy act wasn't fooling her.

"Right. You can goal keep when he shoots, and vice versa."

God no. "I was thinking more along the lines of me shooting from a particular spot and then Rome having to take the same shot."

Amelia's eyes lit up. "Like that basketball game H.O.R.S.E.? I like it! Just promise me you'll beat him."

Jade smiled, but sometimes, it sure felt like Amelia had it out for the guy. "I'll do my best."

"You always do."

Which was sort of why she was here. "I actually need to talk to you about something other than soccer."

"Sure. Close the door. Sit."

Jade did neither. "It's not really a big deal. You asked me to keep you posted on my job hunt, so I am. I have an interview with the Cleveland Metro Schools."

Amelia look disappointed. "That was fast."

It felt kind of fast to Jade, too. "Well, it's just an interview. And even if I get the job, it won't change the fact that school starts at the end of August. I'll still be around here for another six weeks or so."

Believe her, she was going to squeeze everything she could out of these next several weeks. Because between the on-air antics, off-air fireworks, and the playoff football games, this was shaping up to be the best summer of her life.

Amelia nodded, still clearly concerned. "Thanks for letting me know."

"Yep." She started to back away.

"What if I offered you a full-time job?"

Jade's jaw dropped as a bolt of excitement shot through her. This was exactly what Jillian had been talking about. But what if? Once the initial excitement waned, she honestly didn't know. She doubted the job would come with a pension, and it definitely didn't have summers off. And ... she was getting ahead of herself. "*Are* you offering me a full-time job?"

"I'd like to. I really would. But I need to talk to HR and work some things out first. That is, if you're interested."

Was she? Again, she didn't know what would be the right thing to say. The initial bolt of excitement had left her a little jumpy, even as the practical voice in her head said, "Don't be silly. You're a teacher."

It wouldn't hurt to hear Amelia out, though.

• • •

Rome's Twitter feed started blowing up around 1:00 p.m. with news that embattled Boltz coach Frank O'Malley had resigned. There was nothing like being on air when big sports news broke. What a rush! He was still absorbing serious adrenaline when he wrapped up the show and stepped out into the hallway where Jade was waiting.

"That was crazy!" she said, her smile as big as his.

The phones had rung nonstop.

"How about that guy from Ashtabula who said McAllister should take over as head coach? Bet you loved that?"

"I loved it all." Her eyes sparkled in the fluorescent lights.

He should kiss her. Why waste a good adrenaline rush?

He leaned in, only to be stopped by her odd request. "Can we talk?"

Talk? He'd just talked for four hours straight.

He pulled back. "About what?"

Amelia busted out of the studio. "Rome, I need you to get those voiceovers done."

He didn't take his eyes off Jade's startled face. "Okay."

"Now! We were supposed to start running those ads today."

He glanced at Amelia, who was holding the studio door open and tapping her foot. "Fine." He wasn't going to argue with her and ruin a perfectly good day.

"We'll *talk* later," he said to Jade.

"I'll wait in your office."

It was that important?

Two hours later, he made his way back down the hallway, stopping off at Amelia's office first to tell her the precious voiceovers were done.

"She's ready for a full-time hosting gig, and you're the perfect producer for her long-term."

Amelia's voice stopped him in his tracks.

She? The only she he could think of was Jade. So he'd been right. The plan *was* to give Jade her own show. But already? Jesus! What happened to paying dues? He'd started out producing and then spent years subbing for senior on-air personalities before he'd ever gotten a shot at a regular gig. Jade, the math teacher, rolls in and bam! She's ready to headline.

"This has been my plan all along."

As if he needed the confirmation. Jade was just another way for Amelia to make his life miserable. Too bad it sort of backfired. It was hard to be miserable when you enjoyed spending time with the person in question.

He shook his head. Whatever. Amelia could give Jade her own show—as long as it wasn't his.

That thought settled a little heavier than he'd expected it to. What if it *was* his? What if that had been the grand plan? Worse, what if Jade was in on it? Again, he thought about how convenient it was to have a women's football team show up at his remote show the very night he was supposed to give more airtime to women in sports.

The flashing thought renewed his suspicions and made him sick. *No. No way.* Jade said so herself. And after this weekend, he'd come to trust her. What possible plan could include helping him out with his family? There was no plan. Jade was not in on some hostile takeover. Absolutely not. This tightening in his chest was pointless.

"I talked to her today," Amelia said. "She's on board."

Fuck. How could he explain that away?

He was vibrating with so much anger, he almost didn't feel his phone quivering in his front pocket. One look at the screen and all he could think was, *Speak of the devil.*

Her text was short and sweet:

Where are you?

Getting screwed over, apparently. Which wasn't exactly a surprise coming from Amelia. But from Jade? Getting screwed over by the woman you were screwing was sickeningly ironic.

When he reached his office, she was standing behind his desk with her back to the door, looking at the framed photograph of him and Cleveland Boltz great Bo James. Her long, dark hair was gathered in a rhinestone clip and spilled down her back. And for a second, the ratings, the job, didn't matter. He only wanted to grab hold of that ponytail and pull hard enough to tip her chin and bare her throat to his lips. To taste her skin on his tongue again. To feel her ...

"Oh. Hey." She smiled at him. "I thought you got lost. It took you long enough. How'd the voiceovers go?"

"I don't want to talk about the voiceovers."

She looked confused by his change in tone. "Then what do you want to talk about?"

"Be completely honest with me. Are you here to take my job?"

She rolled her eyes like it was the craziest thing she'd ever heard. "No. Why would you even think that?" She seemed genuine, but maybe she was just a good liar.

"I overheard Amelia talking on the phone to someone. She said some things that made me think the end plan involves you in this office. And me." He hesitated. "Gone. Is that it?"

"God no!" She was around the desk in a blink, standing before him. "Rome, that's not what's going on. Amelia asked me today if I was interested in a full-time job, and I said I'd listen to the offer, but that's it. I tried to tell you earlier. That's why I'm waiting here right now. I don't want your job. I don't even really want a full-time job in radio." Her face wrinkled for a split second. "In fact, I just scheduled an interview with the Cleveland Metropolitan Schools on Thursday."

He didn't know what to believe. He knew what he wanted to believe. He wanted Amelia to be 100 percent to blame for this. But could he risk being that naive considering what was on the line, when he'd only know Jade for a few weeks?

"I promise you." She took his hands in hers. "I'm not here to take your job. I'd be lost without you."

But she was a fast learner, wasn't she? Eventually, she wouldn't need him—for anything.

Keep an eye on this one, Rome. Better yet, keep a little distance. He needed a paycheck more than he needed her pretty promises.

• • •

Jade slam-dunked the teaching interview. Her multicultural upbringing had been the icing on the proverbial cake for a diverse school district.

"I have a good feeling about this," the female superintendent had said. It was a fairly definitive send-off. Which was excellent.

Now Jade could relax. Her rent would be paid with or without Jillian. Umma and Halmoni would be thrilled to hear she was heading back to teaching in the fall. And Rome would be relieved to have concrete proof she wasn't after his job. So why wasn't *she* happier?

It had to be nerves over Saturday's football game. Once a win was in the books, she would be more than happy with her life—she would be satisfied. Until then, she could settle the jitters with a visit to Hindy Hair, where Umma and Halmoni would be ecstatic about the positive interview.

When Jade walked in, Umma's eyes lit up, and the pair of scissors she'd been wielding hit the metal stand beside her. "What a wonderful surprise! We were just talking about you."

Jade had just enough time to nod a greeting at Mrs. Lee, who'd been abandoned in her swivel chair, before Umma wrapped her up in a hug.

"How was the interview?" her mother asked.

"Great!" She said the word with more force than necessary, hoping the meaning would be contagious. "I really think they're going to hire me."

"Of course they are! They would be foolish not to. You are the best teacher in Cleveland."

Jade laughed as she looked into her mother's smiling eyes. "You're my mother. You have to say that." But still it was nice to hear.

"You're the best teacher in Cleveland," Mrs. Lee said with a grin. "And I'm not your mother, so you can believe me."

Sweet. Although, it didn't carry much weight, either. People in this neighborhood stuck together.

"Thank you," Jade said as the door connecting the salon to the house opened, and Halmoni shuffled out.

Jade went to her, helped her over the lip in the linoleum floor, and placed a gentle kiss on her cheek. "Hi, Halmoni."

"Jade got the job," Umma said.

"Well, not yet."

Halmoni patted Jade's hand. "You will. You're smart, patient, and good with children." Her mother and Mrs. Lee agreed.

She was good on the radio, too, apparently. That's why Amelia wanted to offer her a full-time job. But would her family support a radio career if it meant Jade said goodbye to teaching? Not that she was anywhere near as enthusiastic about that idea after Rome's reaction. She didn't want him perpetually side-eyeing her, thinking she was scamming with Amelia to take his job.

"Cleveland schools pay well," Umma said. "With full benefits and a pension."

"That's wonderful," Mrs. Lee said.

"You'll never find yourself cleaning other people's toilets as long as you're teaching."

"I know, Umma."

It got quiet, a nod to the hard years after her father had left, when the three of them had pulled together to do whatever it took to get by. Cleaning and ironing weren't easy jobs, but they were honest jobs, and Jade had the sudden urge to defend all the hours Halmoni had spent scrubbing and washing.

"But, thank God for cleaning other people's toilets, because it put you through beauty school, right?"

Her mother nodded thoughtfully. "It did."

Jade squeezed Halmoni's arm in a sign of solidarity. "Together we accomplished a lot."

"That's Korean, you know?" Mrs. Lee asked. "These American mothers push their children to be self-sufficient, and then they wonder why those children aren't around to help them out later on." She shook her head. "You have a responsibility to your family. At least you do in Korea."

It was no surprise that Umma and Halmoni agreed. They had definitely raised Jade that way, but she'd mostly thought it had been the result of necessity.

"You don't have to worry about our Jade," Umma said. "She's got her head screwed on straight."

Jade exhaled. That was why this teaching job was so important. After everything they'd been through, she wanted her mother and grandmother to have peace. Their happiness was her happiness. To a certain degree. To what degree was exactly what she'd been trying to determine these past six months living on her own. For all the Korean family values that had been instilled in her, she was still half American.

The bell above the door chimed, and she turned to see an attractive man walk in. He was definitely all Korean. Black shiny hair. Creamy flawless skin. A gleaming smile. Dressed in a beige suit, he looked like a designer menswear ad. And he had the height. At least six feet of it.

This was the elusive total package Umma and Halmoni had been searching for. This was Mrs. Lee's grandson, wasn't it?

"Bon-Hwa!" Mrs. Lee was out of her chair and rushing the door. "You're back."

A few seconds later, Jade was being shoved toward the handsome stranger, who was introduced as Mrs. Lee's grandson, the pilot.

"Nice to meet you." She smiled up at him and extended her hand.

He took it softly, smoothly in his, and she felt ... nothing. Certainly nothing that led her to believe she'd feel a similar gut-punch lust like she'd felt when she'd first kissed Rome.

Scruffy jawed, gravelly voiced, sexy grinned, jumping-to-the-worst-conclusions Rome. She'd come to know him pretty well these last few weeks, but still she didn't dare imagine him being anything more than the guy she'd kissed on the steps to prove a point, the guy who was now a colleague with benefits. If Rome walked into this salon today, her mother and grandmother would take one look at him and see Jade's American father—only shorter. Then where would they be?

"Very nice to meet you," Bon-Hwa said.

Encouraging, satisfied sounds filled the air around them as the matchmakers gave their approval. She'd been through this so many times before, she just went with the flow.

"I'm so glad you two finally got to meet," Mrs. Lee said. "We've been waiting for this."

Didn't she mean planning for this? Bon-Hwa walking in while she was here was probably a setup.

Umma pushed Jade even closer. "You should show him around while he's here."

Jade hated the hard sell. It made her look and feel desperate. Besides, total package or not, she wasn't exactly interested in him.

But ... Halmoni, who'd spent twenty-five blissful years married to a good Korean man before she was shattered by his death, looked so damn happy.

Jade bit her bottom lip and snuck another look at Bon-Hwa. He definitely looked like the right guy. Maybe her interest would grow if they spent more time together. Maybe that kiss would be explosive.

"I do make a pretty mean tour guide," she said.

He smiled. "Excellent. How about Saturday?"

Not in a million years. "I have an important football game this Saturday. How long are you in town?"

He looked at her funny, like maybe he didn't understand her English even though he seemed to speak the language perfectly.

Umma dismissed the scheduling conflict with a wave of her hand. "You can spend Sunday together."

"That sounds good," Mrs. Lee said. "We have nothing planned."

Halmoni nodded emphatically.

Bon-Hwa seemed to think it over, and then after looking at his grandmother said, "It works for me."

Jade wondered if it was a scheduling conflict that made him hesitate or the same unwanted pressure she was under. Apparently, they could talk about that on Sunday, because it was unanimous ... almost. Behind her smile, Jade wished for a graceful, easy way out of this group decision, but she knew better. They were a tough crowd, and she wasn't going to disappoint them.

"You can play soccer on Saturday and then come with me on Sunday. How does that sound?" he asked.

Soccer? She shook her head and almost laughed when she heard a few gasps. "I play American football. Tackle football."

He looked like she was talking in a foreign language again.

Speaking her mind inside the station must've had a funny effect on her out here, because she randomly said, "You know what? I can't commit to Sunday." Umma's disappointed sigh cut right through her, so she backtracked a bit. "Not yet. If we lose on Saturday, I won't be very good company."

The Clash wouldn't lose. Jade refused to even think that way. Which meant she was going to have to come up with some other excuse to get herself off the hook without disappointing everyone else in this room.

Or just go, said the voice in her head. It was easier that way.

"I didn't know women played American football," Bon-Hwa said. "Then again, I don't know much about sports in general. They don't really interest me."

So much for being the total package.

Chapter Eleven

Rome was under no obligation to be at this game. He didn't owe Jade anything. He hadn't lost any more bets. In fact, he still wasn't sure what to make of Jade and the whole full-time radio thing. But ever since July Fourth, Tess had been asking about her nonstop, and it had been a while since he and Tess had had their own day.

He'd promised himself to keep some distance from Jade, and twenty-six rows up definitely qualified. Hell, she didn't even know he was here, and he intended to keep it that way.

"I have to pee really bad." Tess fidgeted in her seat beside him.

It was a long way down, and there were only five minutes left in a back-and-forth, conference championship game, but when natured called, you listened.

"Okay, kiddo." Hopefully, he could walk her down, send her in, and stand where he could still see the game. "Let's go." He held on to her hand and made their excuses as he edged out of the packed row and down the steps.

At the bottom, he turned left and weaved through the crowd. Restrooms were probably by the concession stand.

"You hanging in there?" He glanced back at Tess, who was walking funny but nodding. "Almost there."

Farrell with the carry. First and ten Clash.

The announcer's voice infiltrated the buzz of the crowd, and Rome slowed his pace to catch the next play. He scanned the line of scrimmage until his eyes locked on to the scuffed-up red helmet in the center. A clash of equipment sent an echo through the stadium, but the ball didn't soar, and the running back didn't bolt. A sense of foreboding filled the humid air.

He veered a little closer to the fence for a better look, and that's when he saw the scramble. Fumble on the snap. *Shit.*

"Pelicans' ball," the announcer said.

The crowd groaned, and Rome swore under his breath as he led Tess toward the concession stand.

"What happened?" she asked. "Why is everyone booing?"

"Somebody dropped the ball."

"And that's bad?"

"Really bad." He just hoped it was the quarterback's mistake, not Jade's, because carrying that kind of weight through the rest of the game sucked. And if they lost ... He could only imagine how much she would beat herself up over it. That was one thing that definitely wasn't determined by gender.

Once Tess was safely inside the women's room, Rome wandered back to the chain-link fence that separated the running track from the field. He watched the Pelicans steamroll the Clash defense until the ball sat in the red zone.

He leaned on the fence and roughed a hand over his face, surprised by how much one measly fumble bothered him. He wasn't vested in this team. He wasn't vested in their center. He definitely didn't want to be vested in her after what had happened on Monday.

Touchdown Pelicans.

He kicked the chain link, then searched the sidelines for a glimpse of Jade. Nothing. The area was thick with players in the midst of the switch to special teams.

"Can I get a hotdog?" Tess appeared at his side looking hopeful.

"You bet." He reached into his pocket, and pulled out a ten-dollar bill.

"I have my own money." She held up her purse. "From my job."

He smiled as he stuffed the ten back into his jeans. "Suit yourself."

A sense of pride puffed out his chest, when she walked away, a bounce in her step. It was nice to see her pushing for more independence.

The extra point is good. The Pelicans lead the Clash 28 to 21.

Rome frowned. Four minutes on the clock. Plenty of time to fix this downward spiral. He saw Jade running onto the field, and he willed her to forget about the fumble. "Let's go, baby! Clean slate."

He held his breath through the kickoff and then again through the snap. The QB dropped back and let loose a thirty-yard bomb that was reeled in by a wide receiver, who picked up ten more yards on the carry.

Rome clapped, fired off another "Let's go," and glanced at the clock again. "Plenty of time. Plenty of time."

"For what?" Tess was at his side again. Her mouth full of hotdog.

"For two touchdowns. We'll get one here, and then we'll get the ball back and get another."

"We will?" She looked confused.

"Well, not you and me. Them, but that's who we're rooting for, so I'm talking like we're all on the same team."

She still looked confused.

He laughed. "Just eat your hotdog."

"It's good!" The proof was in her ketchup-laden grin.

Another snap. The clash of pads and the sound of conflict drew his attention back to the field, where the running back carved a path through the Pelicans' defense and straight to the five-yard line.

"Beautiful!" He fist pumped.

"Rome Rizzelli? Is that you?"

He looked behind him to see a chubby guy stuffing his face with nachos.

"I thought you hated women's football," the guy said. "I guess I shouldn't be surprised now that the Asian chick has weaseled her way in there. Goddamned political correctness."

She was *half Asian*, and that had nothing to do with her getting the job.

"Listen, buddy ..." But a ruckus on the field clipped Rome's words.

There was shoving on the sidelines. From this vantage point, Rome couldn't tell who started it. He couldn't tell if punches were actually thrown.

"Get out of my way, retard. I can't see."

Time stopped. The only noise Rome heard was the sound of his blood boiling up to his ears. He turned and got in the guy's face. "What the fuck did you say?" But just as quickly and harshly as he'd said it, he warned the guy not to say the word again. "Apologize to my sister right now, and you won't leave on a stretcher with the rest of those nachos lodged in your throat."

"Hey, hey!" The guy backed up a little. "I'm just saying the truth. Isn't that what you always say? 'It's the truth. You don't like it you can ...'"

Rome grabbed Tess's hand and got the hell out of there. He wasn't interested in having that stupid tagline thrown back at him as justification for acting like an idiot.

"You've gone soft, Rizzelli!" the guy yelled. "And that *is* the truth."

Yeah, well ... Rome thought about it for a few angry seconds. He supposed he'd always been soft when it came to his family. That was just a side of him few people got to see. Suddenly, he wanted that to change.

"Hey ..." He pulled Tess off to the side well away from the man and looked her dead in the eyes. "Are you okay?"

She nodded. "Are you mad?"

"Yes, I'm mad."

"Don't be." She wrapped her arms around his waist and hung on for dear life.

Heavy emotions warred in his chest, and he knew his sister deserved better than a brother who assembled an army of closed-minded idiots.

"Are we going back to our seats?" Tess asked, releasing him.

He had no desire to be part of a crowd that included that loser. "No. We're going to stay down here and get a better look at this touchdown."

They reached the end zone in time to see MJ sneak across the goal line for a TD.

Rome whooped, and Tess looked at him funny.

"What?" He shrugged it off.

She giggled. "That was a funny sound."

He whooped again just to see her smile.

She whooped, too.

They laughed through the kickoff. But the minute the Pelicans had the ball in Clash territory, he was gnawing the inside of his cheek and thinking about Jade. They could not lose this game.

When the Pelicans were forced to punt, a "hell yeah" rocketed out of Rome's mouth. A second later, the parrot beside him hollered the same thing.

He pulled Tess into a brief side hug. This had been quite the day.

Usually when they went out, they went to the movies or the arcade. Never sporting events. After seeing how much she enjoyed this—how much he enjoyed this—that was definitely something else that was going to change. He was not going to let a sour run-in with some blowhard idiot ruin it.

"Here we go," he said. "This is where we win the game." And better yet, that fumble would become ancient, irrelevant history.

"Are you going to make that funny sound again?" Tess looked hopeful.

"Absolutely! And you better do it with me."

But the return was weak. Five measly yards. His mother could do better than that, and *she* had balance issues.

"Let's go!" he yelled.

Tess echoed the sentiment.

Snap. MJ handed off to the running back, who dodged and drilled four defenders on her way to a twenty-yard pick up.

"Here we go!" he yelled.

"Here we go," Tess said.

He smiled, even as he did the math in his head and realized time was running out.

Thirty seconds left.

Snap the ball, baby.

In a blink, the ball was in the QB's hands. Another blink, and the running back was in hand-off range. But the transition wasn't smooth. The ball bobbled, hitting the turf amid deafening groans. Again.

"Something bad happened," Tess said.

All he could do was nod and pray.

In the midst of the on-field crowd, he glimpsed number sixty reacting first. Jade's hands were on the wobbling pigskin.

"Grab it, baby! Grab it!"

She nearly fell when a defender dove for the ball and took out her legs, but instead of collapsing in the pile quickly forming at her feet, she lifted the ball and high stepped out of the chaotic heap, cutting right, banking left, and rolling twice before she shook off the last defender.

"No way!" Nothing but green between Jade and the end zone. "Are you kidding me?" He grabbed onto Tess and pointed in the direction of the action. "Jade's going to score!"

It wasn't every day a lineman, er, linewoman scored a touchdown.

"Touchdown Clash!" the announcer screamed, and the crowd went wild.

"Hell yeah!" Rome added a fist pump for good measure.

"Hell yeah," Tess repeated. "Can we whoop now?"

He grinned at his sister. "Yes, we can. On the count of three. One. Two. Three."

She whooped before he did, and the skin around her eyes crinkled until she was nothing but lids and a massive, gummy smile.

As he pulled his sister into a hug, he realized something. Of all the games he'd covered, of all the Super Bowl, World Series, and Stanley Cup wins he'd been privy to see, this barely pro women's game just became his hands-down favorite.

• • •

Jade busted out of the locker room celebration early so she could meet up with Umma and Halmoni. Family first; friends later.

The Clash had won the championship—on her touchdown. *My touchdown.* Never in a million years would she have expected to recover a fumble in such a critical part of the game.

"There's our winner!" Umma said.

The tall guy behind Halmoni distracted Jade. *Bon-Hwa.* She had no idea he was going to be here. He wasn't even into sports.

"Congratulations," he said.

Halmoni grabbed her hands and pulled her into a hug. "You scored the points!"

Jade chuckled. "Not all of them."

"The most important ones." It was a low, deep voice that she'd grown increasingly preferable toward these last few weeks.

She broke Halmoni's hug to find Rome standing there.

"You came," she said with a smile, never imagining he would. He hadn't said anything about coming all week—even when she'd mentioned the game.

He tipped his head in the direction of Tess, who was by his side. "Your biggest fan has been wanting to see you in action."

How sweet!

"Hi!" Tess squinted a smile and waved.

Jade took a step toward the young woman. "I'm so glad you guys came! Did you have fun?"

"We whooped!" Tess looked at Rome expectantly.

He chuckled. "No. Not now. We'll do it for her later."

"Do what?" They had her curious.

"Jade?"

Umma. Jade hesitated. How exactly was she going to explain this?

Rome glanced beyond her, and his face wrinkled. Because of Bon-Hwa? Probably. Who'd invited the guy anyway?

She turned to her family, took a few steps to the side, and gestured toward Rome and Tess. "This is Rome Rizzelli, my colleague from the radio station, and this is his sister, Tess."

Halmoni looked unimpressed. Umma looked ... suspicious, like she was with most American men.

"Rome and Tess, this is my mother, my grandmother, and ... a family friend, Bon-Hwa."

The greetings were unenthusiastic all the way around. Great. Not exactly the kind of interaction you wanted to be having on the heels of a championship win.

"Thanks for coming," she said to all of them, not sure how to end this gracefully.

"We should go," Umma said. Sharp and to the point.

So much for graceful.

It made Jade want to say "then, go ahead," but the words caught on a lump of the usual guilt in her throat. Postgame had always been Umma and Halmoni's time.

"We probably should," she said. But, ugh! It felt so meek.

For crying out loud, she was allowed to have colleagues and friends. Disgust displaced the guilt, and Jade turned defiantly to Rome and Tess. "You know what? You guys should come with us. We're going to get ice cream."

"I like ice cream," Tess said.

But Rome frowned as he looked behind Jade again. "Tess is lactose intolerant. We'll pass." He placed a hand on his sister's shoulder.

Jade brushed off the disappointment. "Okay. I'm really glad you guys were here."

Rome nodded, and a soft smile parted his lips. "It was a great game. Actually, it was extraordinary."

A joyful laugh bubbled up, and Jade had the fleeting thought to run to him, throw her arms around his neck, and seal the win with a kiss, but instead she just smiled. "You'd better watch yourself, Rizzelli. People might start accusing you of being a women's football fan."

"I've been accused of much worse. And I've probably deserved it."

The eye contact was intense. The pull to him even stronger.

"Jade?" Halmoni interrupted.

And as much as Jade wanted to stay with Rome, she flinched. How could she defend what was going on between her and Rome if she didn't even know what to call it? Now was definitely not the time and place.

"I'll see you around." She waved at Tess, smiled at Rome, and then halfheartedly joined her family.

Umma and Halmoni parted like a biblical sea, ushering Jade and Bon-Hwa into the center.

Umma slipped her arm through Jade's and brought her closer. "That one doesn't know how to shave—just like your father. He looks like trouble." Umma made a face full of disgust. "And, he's so short."

"*That one* is a coworker," Jade said in hushed tones, only wanting this conversation to end.

"You were great," Bon-Hwa said. "I mean I'm assuming you were great. I didn't understand most of it. But you scored, and that's excellent. Right?"

She glanced up at him, taking in his chiseled, clean-shaven face and practiced smile. So pretty. Too pretty. Apparently, that was enough to make her mother think *this one* wasn't trouble.

But trouble was a funny thing. It wasn't always as bad as it looked. She thought back to Rome ... with Tess ... at this game, and a warm feeling fizzed in her chest.

What if there was a way to make her family see what she saw? Would she be willing to push for something more with Rome then?

Chapter Twelve

"Drink, drink, drink, drink!"

Jade downed the shot and wiped her mouth with the back of her hand. She was going to pay for this in the morning, but championships only came round once a year. And championship wins were even rarer.

"Two more!" Jillian yelled.

"No! No, I'm done."

"Come on! Six shots for the six points you scored."

"Two more will kill me. I'm not sure I can get off this barstool as it is." Yep. She was slurring her words.

Thank God she didn't live at home anymore. If she stumbled in like this, Umma and Halmoni would be convinced she was doomed to be a drunk like her dad.

The phone beside her lit up, and Tanya took advantage of Jade's slower reaction time. "Who's Bon-Hwa?"

Jade stared off into space. "Tall, dark, and Korean."

"Yum!" Jillian reached for the phone. "What did he say?"

"He says, 'I hope you're enjoying your evening with friends. If you feel like doing something tomorrow, let me know. I'm here.'"

Tanya nodded. "He sounds nice."

Jillian made a gagging sound. "He sounds lonely and desperate. Besides, nice guys won't push you up against the wall and fuck the hell out of you."

Jade laughed. She couldn't imagine buttoned-up Bon-Hwa doing anything like that. Rome on the other hand ...

"Gimme it." Jillian reached for the phone again. "I'm going to respond."

"No!" Jade lunged, too.

MJ jumped between them. "Neither one of you is going to respond."

"It's my phone."

"You're drunk."

"Am not." Her elbow slipped off the edge of the bar, prompting teasing from the teammates around her.

"But if I don't respond, he's going to think I'm being rude."

MJ studied her closely. Actually, *three* MJ's studied her closely. "You do know you don't have to respond to texts right away. There's no rule anywhere that says that."

Maybe not, but it seemed like the right thing to do. And considering it was Bon-Hwa, it definitely was the thing her mother and grandmother would expect her to do. But she could probably say "screw it" to the expectations, considering she was now drunk hanging on to the bar. Nice, huh? This double life was really getting to her.

"Respond in the morning when you're sober," Tanya said. "You can tell him you lost your phone if it makes you feel better."

"It won't, because that's a lie."

"Fine." Tanya stuck the phone into her back pocket. "I'll hide it. Then you won't be lying."

Jade attempted to prop her elbow on the bar again. Success!

"Do you want to do something with him tomorrow?" MJ asked.

"I don't know." He was sweet at the ice cream parlor. Even insisted on paying for everything. He got along with Umma and Halmoni. He said the right things, looked the right way. But ... she didn't feel anything. And he didn't like sports!

Jillian rolled her eyes. "Give her back her phone so she can talk to the guy and figure this out."

Tanya shook her head and backed away, pulling MJ with her. "Alcohol clouds the mind."

"Alcohol is a truth serum," Jillian said.

"Sober up a little. Then I'll think about it." Tanya and MJ slipped into a larger group of teammates who were gathered around the pool table.

Jillian dropped to the stool beside Jade. "Listen to me. I know what's going on here." She may have slurred a few words, too. "Juggling guys isn't easy for a seasoned pro, let alone a goodie-goodie like you. That's why I think you should text Tall, Dark, and Korean and decide if he's worth the aggravation. If he's not, then let yourself off the hook." Jillian offered her phone. "Here. Text him from my phone, and invite him back to our place. I won't be there. Carter is picking me up in a half hour." She grinned.

Jade shook her head as she stared at Jillian's phone. "That's a bad idea." She could barely keep her eyes open.

"It's a great idea. You can tell a lot about a guy by the way he acts when you're drunk. He'll be himself, because he'll think you won't remember."

"I won't."

"You'll remember bits and pieces. You'll remember the important stuff—as long as you don't pass out first." Jillian rocked into her, nudging her with a shoulder. "Seriously. What's his number?"

Jade didn't know Bon-Hwa's number, but oddly enough, she knew Rome's. All the back and forth arranging appointments with Tag had burned the number into her brain.

She pushed Jillian's phone away. "I don't want to text Bon-Hwa."

Jillian looked disappointed.

"But ... I do want to text someone else." Crap. She hadn't meant to say that out loud.

Jillian grinned and handed over her phone. "Rome would totally fuck you against the wall."

Another shocked laughed flew past Jade's lips. "That's not why I'm texting him."

"Then why are you smiling like that?"

"Because I'm drunk, and you're crazy."

Jillian laughed. "Awesome things happen when those two things combine."

Horrible things happened, too. Still, Jade typed in Rome's number and held her breath. "I don't even know what to say to him."

"Gimme the phone," Jillian said. "I'll handle it."

• • •

"*Say Yes to the Dress* is on!" Tess said it with enough urgency to make even Rome want to rip the remote from his mother's hand and change the channel so Tess didn't miss a thing.

"No! I'm watching this." His mother's attention remained on the television screen, where a tall, skinny chick with purple hair and the ugliest dress he'd ever seen strutted down a runway. "Use the TV in Rome's bedroom."

Tess looked at him hopefully.

That meant he'd be stuck watching *America's Next Top Model* reruns with his mother, but ... "Sure." He was used to it, and it put a smile on Tess's face. It was also much better than listening to them bickering.

He would just sit here and play around with his phone, or ... he could go out for an hour or two. Do something. Sit at a bar and watch some baseball like he did whenever he needed some time away from the house. Maybe he would meet somebody. But for some reason, blowing off a little steam all boozed up in the backseat of a car didn't have the same allure as it used to.

No, tonight, he'd been itching to text, talk to, and see somebody *in particular.*

He hadn't stopped thinking about Jade since the game. And every time he thought about her, he thought about the smarmy Asian dude with the perfect hair. Something in the guy's predatory smile raised Rome's territorial alarm. *Family friend, my ass.* He was into her. Of course he was. What wasn't there to be into?

Jade had said she wasn't looking for anything serious, but that guy had looked too serious for his own good.

"Do you know how to tooch?" his mother asked.

"What?" he looked up at her.

"Tyra says it's all about the tooch."

He glanced at the television to see the models sticking their asses out in an exaggerated fashion. "What the hell is a tooch?"

His mother laughed and laughed.

Finally, Rome had no choice but to laugh, too. He didn't hear that often, and it sounded good. Good enough that maybe he would just stay here after all.

He reached out to set his phone on the coffee table, but it lit up in his hand. An incoming text from a number he didn't recognize:

Have you ever had sex against a wall?

Talk about random. His eyes widened, and he typed:

Who is this?

He only had a handful of ex-girlfriends from way back when—none of them daring or outspoken enough to send a text like that. And he never gave out his cell phone number to one-night stands. Who the hell would be ballsy enough to text something like this?

There was no response. The longer he sat there staring at the crazy question, the more he suspected it was a wrong number. Too bad. His night had finally stared to get interesting.

The phone vibrated again:

It's me, Jade.

He wrinkled his face. Somebody was messing with him. Probably somebody from the station. He swiped his finger to delete the message, but then thought better of it. What if it really was Jade? She was no doubt out partying with her teammates.

Maybe she'd had just enough to stoke that little devil who'd been gutsy enough to kiss him on the stairs. He grinned, but still he hesitated to reply. Would two beers get her there?

Rome: Whose number is this? What happened to your phone?

Again, the return message took longer than it should have, and in that time, he wondered which jokester at the station would want to punk him badly enough to pretend to be Jade.

I'm using Jillian's phone.

Rome would buy that.
Another text popped up:

We're out celebrating.

Which was exactly what he'd thought. Now, what was he going to do about it?
He supposed it all depended on her answer to this:

Would you like to have sex against a wall, Jade?

The little thought bubbles that told him she was reading his message or typing one of her own seemed to go on and on, ramping up his expectations.

Maybe.

He laughed and ignored his mother when she shushed him. It had taken an awful long time for Jade to send that one word, but her next message came much quicker:

You should meet me at my place.

Yes. Yes, he should.

Fifteen minutes later, he had his mother and sister settled for the next couple of hours without him. He promised to be back to get them both ready for bed, and then he booked it over to Jade's. All the while, he wondered if it was physically possible for his messed up pec to indulge in acrobatic sex. But it was worth a try.

He took the stairs to her apartment by two and knocked on the door with vigor.

She answered naked.

Clutching his heart, he rushed inside. "That's what I call a greeting."

"Hi." Her smile was sleepy, and her steps toward him were wobbly.

She was drunker than he expected.

The minute her soft body was wrapped in his arms, he smelled the booze. Talk about a mood killer. He dropped his open mouth to her silky shoulder and groaned. She could barely stand, and he hated to admit her weak knees had nothing to do with him.

Tonight wasn't going to happen.

She rubbed against him as she yanked at his T-shirt. "Which wall?"

He dragged his lips up her neck to her earlobe and groaned again. "No wall."

"Why?" She pulled back and looked at him. "Oh! Oh my God! Your muscle tear. I forgot."

She slurred her words, which was further proof that he shouldn't look between them, where her glorious body was willing and waiting.

"You forgot because you're plastered," he said. "What happened to your two-drink maximum?"

"I was celebrating."

"Mmm hmm. A hell of a lot by the looks of it."

"And now we can celebrate together." She swiped her hand brazenly over the bulge in his jeans.

He pushed it away. Gently. "Listen, we can celebrate another night."

"No!" She looped her arms around his neck and went for his mouth.

He opened wide, letting her tongue slide inside, tasting the liquor on her lips. Hard liquor, when he knew she was a light beer kind of girl.

As much as he wanted this, he knew better, so he broke the sloppy kiss. "You need someone to take care of you, not take advantage of you."

She shook her head wildly. "I *want* someone to take advantage of me."

And that was the problem. She wanted *someone. Anyone.* It was the booze talking. He'd been there. For all he knew, she'd texted the other guy first, and then when he'd been too serious for a quickie, she'd called Rome, who had "quickie" written all over him. But not tonight. No thanks. Rome didn't feel like being the rebound when it came to Jade.

That old warning about keeping a reasonable distance replayed in his head. It really was the smartest thing.

"Come on," he said. "Let's get you dressed and into bed."

She booed.

"You'll thank me later."

"No, I won't." Her roving hands tried to convince him of that all the way down that hall.

Once they were in her bedroom, she flounced on the bed. "Come here."

Hell, no. Not while she was naked. He dug into the drawers beside him, pulled out the least sexy thing he could find—a black

T-shirt and fuzzy cream leggings—and threw them at her. "Put those on."

She cackled.

"What's so funny?"

"These are thermal underwear." She held up the leggings. "I wear them skiing, not to bed." She tossed them aside.

"Fine. I'll get something else." He reached for the drawer.

"This is good enough."

When he turned back around, she was dressed in the little black T, which barely covered her ass.

"Come here," she said again, curling up on the bed and smiling sweetly.

That damn T-shirt rode high on her thigh, and he knew he was doomed if he did as she said, so he modified her request. "I'll lay with you for a few minutes. Just until you fall asleep. And only if you get—and *stay*—under those covers."

Once she obliged, he settled beside her—on top of the comforter—and scooped her up in his arms. Her soft breath tickled his neck, and the flowery scent of her silky hair invaded his nose. A few minutes like this, and he was so damn content he wanted to fall asleep.

The silence lingered between them until she asked, "What is this?"

"This?" He adjusted his grip on her shoulder. "This is me being chivalrous. Shocking, huh?"

She shook her head against his chest. "No. I mean. What is going on between us? I thought it was just fun. Just sex."

A lump formed in his throat. "It is. But not when you're drunk. Don't worry. You'll be sober tomorrow," he teased. "We can pick up where we left off."

She laughed a little harder than usual thanks to the booze. She snorted, too.

He strummed a gentle rhythm on her arm beneath her T-shirt's sleeve and smiled at the ceiling. *Be honest, Rome.* Sex or no sex, this wasn't what he'd been gunning for tonight.

"You're not trouble," Jade whispered almost defiantly, pulling him out of his thoughts.

He debated asking what had prompted such a declaration. "Well, that might depend on who you ask."

"My mother thinks you're trouble because you remind her of my dad."

"I remind her of an alcoholic abuser. Nice."

"Well, you're American. My dad is American. She has the same opinion of most American men."

"And you don't?"

"I don't know. I keep trying to prove her wrong. I guess I want to believe as bad as he was, there was something decent inside of him."

He admired her optimism. "Alcohol makes people do some pretty shitty things. I'm not making excuses for him. I'm just saying. Maybe he was a different guy when he was sober."

"Two sides," she said sleepily.

"Two sides," he echoed. On air. Off air. How did you merge the two?

"I have two sides."

He craned his neck so he could see her face. "I know you do. I met one side on the stairs at Ballers', and I met the other side today at the stadium. What's the deal with the family friend?"

"Who? Bon-Hwa? My mother likes him."

Rome nodded. "But I'm assuming that's not *her* boyfriend."

Jade chuckled. "No. She would like him to be my boyfriend."

He tried really hard not to care, but still he held her a little closer. "Do you like him?" So what if he was fishing? He was pretty certain she wouldn't remember any of this come morning.

"He's okay," she said. "He's definitely not as hot as you."

Rome grinned at the ceiling. "That's good to know."

"He says he wants to see me, but I don't want to see him."

The grin died on a pulse of Rome's cheek. "That might be hard considering he's a family friend."

"He's not really. I didn't know what to call him. He's my neighbor's grandson. He's visiting from Seoul. I met him the other day at my mother's beauty shop when I stopped by to tell them about my interview."

Rome wondered when the Seoul train would leave. Not soon enough for him. He tightened his grip on Jade's shoulder and pulled her even closer. "How'd your interview go?"

"Great."

Except she didn't sound great.

"I'm pretty sure they're going to hire me," she said, the disappointment apparent.

"You don't want to be hired?"

She took so long to answer he thought she might've fallen asleep.

"I do," she said. "My mother and grandmother are really excited."

Two sides. "Yeah, but are you excited?"

She wrapped an arm around his waist and nuzzled her face against his neck. "I'm just tired. Thanks for coming over tonight."

"You bet." He stared at the ceiling as her breathing deepened and her body molded to his.

How had they gone from texts about sex against the wall to this? Whatever this was.

What is this? Her original question lingered in his head. He had an answer now. *This* was a problem.

She was young, five years younger than him, and even though she'd said she didn't want anything serious, she would. Look how comfortable she was with this. But Rome Rizzelli was a one-man show. His personal life didn't leave room for a serious relationship, and the ranch-style home he shared with his mother and sister wasn't big enough for two families.

He rarely wished for a different kind of life, because wishing was a waste of time. But tonight, he had some time to spare. In the quiet, he closed his eyes and admitted if he had a different kind of life, he wouldn't mind having Jade in it.

Chapter Thirteen

Jillian had been right. Despite the alcohol, Jade absolutely, positively remembered the important stuff from Saturday night. She'd spent most of Sunday in bed, nursing a wicked hangover and remembering Rome being the perfect gentleman. He'd respected her and held her sweetly as she drifted off to sleep. He'd talked to her and listened to her. All of that made her feel safer and warmer than she'd ever felt. And now, here it was Monday morning, and she couldn't shed the glow. It didn't matter how often he shaved or how tall he was or how terrible her mother assumed he would turn out to be, Jade knew who he was, and he was wonderful.

She didn't want it to be just sex anymore. She was ready to take a stab at something more serious. That both excited and scared the hell out of her. What was she supposed to do next? Tell him? Tell him what? It wasn't like she loved him.

Her chest squeezed. She *did not* love him. No. God, no. She was way ahead of herself. And that's why she wasn't saying anything. Not yet. She needed to figure out exactly what she wanted out of this and how she was going to convince a man who didn't want anything serious to take a chance on her. But first, she had a show to do.

At the bottom of the third hour, during a commercial break, Jade took her usual seat inside the studio across the table from Rome. He had a fresh cup of coffee in his hand and a smile on his face.

"Good afternoon," he said.

"Good afternoon, you."

"What are you talking about today?"

She glanced at her laptop screen. "Trade deadline."

"Riveting." He pressed the cup to his lips, but didn't take a drink. "I thought maybe you'd be talking about your weekend."

Sure. Why not? she thought sarcastically. She'd been thinking about it nonstop.

She grinned. "I don't think listeners want to hear about how you tucked me in."

His eyes deepened to the sexiest shade of green. "That's not what I was referring to."

"Ah. My bad. Then trade deadline it is." She reached for her headphones just as Amelia and a newly hired assistant producer reappeared in the control booth to count down the return from commercial break.

At the end of the lead-in music, Rome set his coffee aside and focused on his laptop. "Welcome back, everybody. We're going to be switching gears here. Jade Wren is with me in the studio, and she has a lot to talk about. Women usually do." He raised his brows at her overtop his screen, and she could tell that he was smiling.

She didn't hesitate to interrupt him. "I don't know about that. You seem to be the one doing all the talking around here."

He chuckled. "Not for the next fifteen minutes. In fact, for the next fifteen minutes, I'm going to be pretty damn quiet doing something I never thought I would do."

She eyed him up. "What's that?"

"I'm going to be eating crow. With an audience. A couple things happened to me over the weekend that made it pretty clear this has been long overdue." He winked at her. "Now, Jade, why don't you tell everybody what *you* did this weekend."

Well, she'd spent a lot of time thinking about wanting a real relationship with the currently cryptic man sitting across from her after he'd responded to a ridiculous text to have sex against a wall, but that wasn't the kind of conversation you had on air— unless you could put a sports spin on it. She was definitely not that clever, so she stuck with the obvious.

"My football team, the Cleveland Clash, won the FFL championship," she said proudly.

"And how did they win it?"

"We played hard."

"Come on, Jade. There's no room for modesty in my studio. You scored the winning touchdown didn't you?"

She grinned. "I did."

"And that's not all, folks. It was actually a fumble recovery for a touchdown. Did I mention she's a linewoman? What are the odds of that?"

"Slim," she said, reveling in how excited he seemed to be for her.

"Congratulations." His warm, husky voice filled her headset and blanketed her body. "And to anybody out there who saw this amazing game, call in and give Jade the props she deserves."

This was the best job ever.

People did call in. In fact, her fifteen minutes turned into more than a half hour of reliving the highs and lows of the game as if it had been as important as any Super Bowl. When she finally left the studio, she had the biggest smile on her face.

"Can I steal you for a minute?" Amelia closed the control room door behind her and joined Jade in the hall.

"Sure."

"Great. My office, please." Amelia took off in a power walk Jade had come to know well over the last few weeks. "Congratulations on the championship and the touchdown ... and on getting Rome to eat crow and share his show for longer than fifteen minutes." She tossed a smile over her shoulder as she stepped into her office. "That has to feel pretty cool."

"It does."

"I bet this will feel even better." Amelia rounded her desk, opened a folder, and pushed it toward Jade.

A logo featuring a neon lightning bolt behind purple and green text that spelled out "JADED ... with Rome Rizzelli" caught her eye. What in the world?

"I told you I wanted you full time. I cleared it with HR, and this is my official pitch. No more fifteen-minute segments. It's not enough. Today proved that. It also proved you and Rome have way too much chemistry to waste. So, I want you here for every show from start to finish. A true cohosting role with the salary and benefits to reflect it." Amelia offered up a different document, a chart that listed numbers much larger than any Jade could expect from teaching. "You'll work the same morning drive-time hours as Rome, and I'll make sure the remote broadcasts don't conflict with your football schedule. You'll be a pioneer, and you'll have the opportunity to be a voice for millions of female athletes and sports fans. How does that sound?"

Awesome! Working side by side with Rome. Talking sports. Re-creating the magic of the last fifteen minutes five days a week? It was a dream job. The kind of job she never could've imagined two months ago. The kind of job she never knew she wanted.

"I'm ... wow." Jade dropped into the chair beside her. "I'm a little overwhelmed." Everything seemed to be falling into place. A championship. A man. A job.

Amelia's desk phone rang, and she ignored it at first, but then she held up a finger. "I think I know who this is. Give me five minutes. You can stay. And then, when I finish this call, you can tell me you're in."

Amelia was so confident. Jade was, too ... until she thought about it practically speaking. She didn't have a broadcast communications degree. This was a random, lucky shot. What happened if she found herself laid off from this job? She supposed teaching would always be there, and she could fall back on that. But wasn't that saying something? Didn't that mean teaching was a safer bet?

Amid Amelia's conversation about soundboards and engineers, Jade mentally listed off the plusses of teaching: full benefits, a pension, and summers off. Not to mention justification for the degrees her mother had slaved away to pay for. And what about Rome? Did this change things? Maybe it wouldn't be appropriate to pursue something serious if they were working together indefinitely. After all, what if it didn't work out? Could they remain professional?

The longer she stared at the logo with all the letters of her name capitalized and in bold print, the more she felt uncomfortable with the top billing. What would he say about *that*? She'd made the assumption once that he'd known about her being hired. She wasn't going to make that same mistake again. Especially not after he'd accused her of trying to take his job not too long ago. She hadn't been, and this scenario was different—very different. Rome would still have his job if she accepted a full-time cohosting position. In fact, it wouldn't be much different than what had happened on air today. Would it?

Amelia hung up and flashed a confident grin. "I can tell by your face something's bothering you. Tell me your concerns, so I can belittle them."

Where to begin? "I'm a teacher."

"You'll still be a teacher. Only instead of teaching children math, you'll be teaching men that women are knowledgeable sports fans, too."

Yeah, but she didn't really care about other men. "What about Rome?"

Amelia made a face. "You'll be teaching him, too. You'll be teaching him to share."

"Share what?" That deep voice cut through Jade like scalding butter.

She looked over her shoulder and saw Rome poking his head around the doorjamb, and her stomach hollowed out. How was it possible to adore someone so completely for the last two days and suddenly fear him—or at least his reaction? She fought the rising reference to her father. She was not going to go there again, not when she'd spent the weekend convincing herself she was ready to open her heart and take a real relationship risk.

"What the hell is that?" Rome stormed into the room and snatched the folder off Amelia's desk.

"Sit down," Amelia said coolly. "We need to talk."

• • •

Rome refused to sit. He didn't need to talk to anyone. He'd talked enough for one day. Hell, he'd talked himself right into a corner where Jade got top billing. He wasn't stupid. He knew what *JADED … with Rome Rizzelli* meant. To think he'd been snowed again.

He tossed the folder onto Amelia's desk and said, "Whatever you two have planned, count me out."

He made the mistake of looking at Jade. Unlike Amelia, whose bored expression said she'd had her fill of Rome, Jade's face crumpled.

"So what are you saying, Rome?" Amelia asked. "You're ready to leave? I don't see your resignation letter anywhere."

If he had another job waiting? Definitely. Once again, Amelia had him by the balls.

He growled in frustration. "I'll hear you out, but I'm going to stand." He didn't want to sit beside Jade. Breathing her in fucked with his head, like it had this morning in the studio. Like it had Saturday night in her bed.

And now look? *JADED … with Rome Rizzelli*. He looked at the garish logo again. *This* was what he got for letting someone in.

"Fine. Stand." Amelia sucked in a breath through her big mouth, and then let it rip. "Effective immediately, Jade is your full-time cohost, and *Riled Up with Rome* is becoming *JADED ... with Rome Rizzelli*."

"Unbelievable," he said.

Amelia literally clapped. "I know! I think it's brilliant."

Jade didn't move a muscle.

"I thought this was temporary." He directed the statement at Jade, but Amelia answered.

"This is whatever I say it is, and I say it's a top-rated show."

"She's a teacher." He spit out the words Jade had placated him with time and time again, except for Saturday night, when she'd sounded indecisive about the teaching job. He'd known it was a problem them. He just hadn't known how big.

"She's a radio host."

"She's right here," Jade said. "And she hasn't even agreed to this, yet." She glanced back at Rome, and her stoic face twisted. "Why is it so hard for you to believe we could be good together more than a few times a week?"

Hell, he knew they were good together. On and off the air. That wasn't the issue. The issue was ... "Because sooner or later, all good things have to come to an end."

"Cut the condescension, Rome." Amelia glared at him. "She's bigger and stronger than you, remember?"

Of course he remembered. He still had the sore pec to prove it.

"I don't want the job," Jade said, standing. "Actually, I don't want the aggravation."

She sounded sure, but when she looked at him, he saw disappointment in her eyes. It ripped through him. Made him think that he was being an unreasonable asshole again. But there was nothing unreasonable about protecting the career and brand he'd made. He was a one-man show. Besides, Jade had nothing invested in this. She was playing along, having fun, and collecting paychecks. If Amelia's big idea crashed and burned, Jade had a freaking master's degree to land on. What did he have? Two women completely depending on him.

"You're not going anywhere, Jade. Sit down, please." Amelia said the words with a lot more patience than she'd ever shown to Rome. "I'm not finished. With either of you." Then, she turned those cold little eyes on him. "Rome, you might be interested to know that this change comes with a slight pay raise, and it moves you back to drive time."

That socked him for a loop. Six to 10:00 a.m. was his old gig, the gig he'd lost when his ratings had slipped, and Amelia's old man had plugged in some syndicated piece of shit that did nothing but pave Barry Vincent's road to the top in gold.

Drive time. Rome didn't want it to matter this much. For one thing, the earlier hours sucked. Up at 3:00 a.m. so he could be ready to go on the air at six? The thought alone was yawn inducing. But the personal satisfaction and the industry prestige could make it worthwhile.

Drive time was a promotion. A big one. It gave him a legitimate shot at being on top of the Cleveland market again.

A smug smile brightened Amelia's face. "That changes things, doesn't it?" She nodded crisply, as if it were a done deal. "Now, Jade, if I can get him to promise there won't be any aggravation, will you take the job?"

He laughed harshly. "Have you met me? Aggravation comes with the package."

Amelia's hard look said she would have the last laugh if he kept acting like a dick. He did not want to go from a shot at drive time to fired.

"Maybe," Jade said. She gave him one of her patented hopeful looks, like the one she'd given him in her apartment when she was drunk and trying desperately to convince him sex was a good idea. Only this time, he crumbled.

"Fine." He rubbed both hands over his face and exhaled. "I can't believe I'm saying this, but *JADED ... with Rome Rizzelli* it is."

"Excellent!" Amelia was the only one who looked and sounded confident and happy.

Meanwhile, Jade's brows pulled together at the top of her nose. All Rome could do was nod in capitulation at his new cohost, because he had a feeling this changed everything.

• • •

Two days after Amelia had dropped her bomb, *JADED ... with Rome Rizzelli* was off and running, and Jade was hoping she hadn't made a terrible mistake.

She blinked the tired burn from her eyes and focused on the time in the lower corner of her laptop screen. *5:55 a.m.* And she'd already been up for two hours.

"I need more coffee," she said.

Rome glanced up at her with the same distance in his eyes that had been there for the last two days. Whenever they talked, he seemed distracted. And the one and only time she'd questioned him directly about it, he'd said nothing was wrong. But she didn't believe him. She had a feeling every time he looked at her, he saw the woman who had slowly but surely changed his show until it was almost unrecognizable. Then again, maybe he was just tired, too.

She was definitely far too exhausted to worry about what she'd been worrying about two days ago. A real relationship with Rome Rizzelli? If she hadn't been so tired, she would've laughed out loud. At this point, the only thing she wanted was to get through the next four hours without falling asleep drooling on her keyboard.

A few minutes and a couple yawns later, new lead-in music filled her headphones. Hard rock, high energy. She cringed. It was too early for this.

But Rome didn't seem to share her sentiments. He came alive, launching into the show with vigor—maybe even more vigor than usual. How was that possible? She'd heard him telling the assistant producer that his alarm had gone off at 3:00 a.m. He was crazy!

"Did you miss me?" The minute he asked the question, the caller queue filled up. Name after name, calling in to welcome back Rome to morning rush radio.

She was happy for him. Mostly. She just wanted him to be happy for her, too.

"I do have a cohost this time," he said, glancing up at her. "Jade Wren. I'm sure you've heard of her by now. She's good."

The words were flattering, but he never looked at her. It was so confusing.

Maybe he would come around.

"Let's take a few calls to kick off the hour."

Just like that. No addressing her directly. No banter. Did he really expect her to sit quietly while he chatted with callers?

"Say something." It was Amelia's voice in her ears. "He's not going to give you airtime, and you shouldn't be waiting for him to. Take it. You're cohosts, Jade. Act like it."

"Mark from Murray Hill, you're live on the air with Rome."

"And Jade," she rushed in.

His beautiful eyes glanced at her overtop his screen. "Mark, what's going on, buddy?"

This felt so wrong. It wasn't at all what Jade had wanted or expected when she'd signed on to cohost.

"Keep pushing," Amelia said.

So Jade did. And by the end of their first four-hour show, things seemed to be a little better.

The next few mornings, Amelia reminded Jade to "hit first," and that it would take time for Rome to relax and get used to the idea of sharing an entire show, especially after he was broadsided with all of these changes. The rationale made sense, but Jade wished he would come around sooner rather than later. She missed the easy banter. She missed *him*.

Finally, she couldn't stand it anymore, and she cornered him.

"Do you hate the show the way it is?" she asked.

"I don't know what to think of it," he said. "Any of it." Before he walked away, he added, "It's not you, though."

"Of course not." How cliché.

At the end of the week, Jade was so disappointed with the lingering distance between them, she called the Cleveland Metropolitan School District for an update on her application— just in case she wanted an "out." She wasn't a quitter, but she wasn't a masochist, either.

Which seemed debatable come Sunday.

After going to church with Umma and Halmoni, Jade convinced herself that scrubbing the beauty shop would be her penance for downplaying the magnitude of *JADED ... with Rome Rizzelli*. She just hadn't been able to find the words to tell them this radio show was supposed to be a new career, not a temporary job.

"I'll be picking up a few more hours at the station," she'd said. But she hadn't mentioned the name change, the pay raise, the benefits package, or the promotional blitzes. All things she should've been gushing about! She'd also done nothing to correct Umma and Halmoni's assumption that the "silly radio show" was still just a way to pass the summer.

If her relationship with them had been different, she would've told them everything, including how disappointed she was with Rome's reaction and the way he was shutting her out. But she bit her tongue, because she knew exactly what they would say. *That man is bad news, and you're a teacher, Jade.* Everything was always so clear cut to them. She was starting to wish it could be clear cut to her, too.

"Don't forget under the dryer chairs." Umma stood on a stool to shine the uppermost corners of a cutting station mirror.

Jade bent to reach the broom beneath the dryer chair. "This is totally backward. The tall person should be doing that. The short person should be doing this."

Umma snorted. "You leave streaks."

God forbid.

Halmoni walked in through the door that led into the house with a laundry basket full of fluffy white towels. She folded while Jade swept and Umma polished. Doo-wop music played softly in the background. For the first time in days, Jade's muscles weren't tense. Being here like this was easy. Everything was routine. The rest of her life could be like this if she left the station and moved back home. Umma and Halmoni would buffer all the hard decisions. But something would be missing. *Someone* would be missing.

Jade banged the broom so hard off the leg of a chair, she nearly broke the handle.

Both Umma and Halmoni reacted, but before they could say anything about her unnecessary aggression, the chime above the door sounded. The shop was closed, but as long as the sun was up, the door wasn't locked.

Jade straightened, pushed the hair off her face, and saw Bon-Hwa smiling at her.

"Morning," he said. "My grandmother told me you were all here, so I thought I'd stop by with these." He held up a bag of bagels and a cardboard box of coffee.

Umma and Halmoni fawned over him. He was dressed in khakis and a pink polo shirt. He'd probably come straight from church. So respectable. Such a gentleman.

Why couldn't she want that? It would make her life so much easier.

He offered to help with the cleaning once the bagels and coffee had been set out on a nearby table. Umma asked him to change lightbulbs in the vanities.

"You don't need a ladder?" Halmoni asked.

"Nope." Bon-Hwa reached over his head and effortlessly unscrewed a bulb.

Umma swooned. "He's so tall."

"And handsome." Halmoni was a terrible whisperer.

Jade saw his grin in the mirror, and she couldn't help but smile, too. Poor guy.

After that, it didn't take long for Umma and Halmoni to find some reason to disappear into the house, leaving Jade and Bon-Hwa alone. How convenient.

"Coffee?" he asked.

"Sure."

They stood side by side at the reception desk where he filled a mug with coffee and she slathered cream cheese on a bagel.

"About last weekend," he said.

Oh my God! She'd forgotten about his text. "I'm sorry! I saw your message Saturday night, when I was out celebrating with the team, and then ... well, I lost my phone." Liar.

He nodded. "I hate when that happens. Did you find it?"

"Yep. And in the chaos, I forgot about your text and then Sunday ..."

"So I'm forgettable?" He looked wounded, but it seemed insincere. "What can I do to change that?" He leaned a little closer. "Because I would really like to spend some time with you."

"You're spending time with me now." Smart ass. Shades of Rome. But she refused to let him weasel his way into this conversation.

"You know what I mean," Bon-Hwa said.

She did. This perfectly coiffed, well-mannered man, who shared her heritage and had earned her mother and grandmother's approval was asking her out. The women in her life were probably watching from a crack in the door, holding their breath, and readying to scream "yes" on her behalf.

It was time she saved them the anxiety.

Chapter Fourteen

Two weeks into the on-air experiment better known as *JADED …
with Rome Rizzelli*, Rome was driving to work under the cover of
darkness and spotted himself illuminated, fourteen feet tall, and
looming over the business loop. He took the next exit and pulled
into a service station to get a better look.

Images of him and Jade anchored the advertisement, which
urged drivers to "Get your game on! Weekdays from 6 to 10 on
Sports Radio 94.7 with Jade and Rome." He had to hand it to
Amelia; she was pulling out all the stops.

As he stood outside his car, admiring the billboard, thinking
about these last two weeks cohosting alongside Jade, he couldn't
ignore how much things had changed. Sixteen days ago, he'd been
holding her in his arms while she'd drifted off to sleep. Two days
later, they'd been hardly speaking, and while it was better now, it
was nowhere near as good as he knew it could be. Why couldn't he
just go with it? 'Cause Rome Rizzelli was a one-man show.

But it was kind of hard to be a one-man show when you had a
cohost. Rome leaned against his car, crossed his arms and thought,
What the hell are you doing, man? Two weeks ago, he'd wanted to
change. Be better. Here was his chance. Wasn't it time to open up
and let her back in? He absentmindedly rubbed a spot above his
heart.

"Rizzelli!"

Rome turned to see none other than Barry Vincent at a nearby
pump. This was not exactly the way he wanted to start his morning,
but he took the high road—surprisingly. "Vincent, what are the
odds?" He didn't go so far as to smile. "How's it going?"

Barry grunted. "Fine. Headed to the station."

"Same." Rome smiled then, a sort of nonverbal jab that he was
back on drive time and gunning for Barry's top spot.

Barry glared at him then looked up at the billboard before leveling his gaze on Rome again. "Don't get too comfortable up there. Remember, I worked with you. You'll do something stupid that costs the station a few grand, and you'll be demoted again. History always repeats itself."

Rome really wanted to hit him, but he stood his ground and simply glanced up at the billboard. "It's gotta be unsettling knowing I'm watching your every move."

Barry slammed the nozzle back into the pump with a clang. "It's gotta be unsettling knowing you're just the bait. I hear the Asian chick's the hook, now. How's it feel to be a worm, Rome?"

"Fuck off, Barry." It was what he should've told the guy ten years ago when Rome had been dragged into Barry's little on-air shenanigans.

"Right back attcha, buddy."

Buddy my ass. He got into his car and peeled out of the lot. Now, more than ever, Rome wanted to bury the son of a bitch in a heap of ratings so high, he would never climb out.

Rome was no worm. He was hook, line, and sinker. If anyone was the bait, it was Jade with her smooth voice, soft laugh, and naive take on the sports world. She brought new, curious listeners in, and he was there waiting to snap them up. He had the experience. He had the seasoned voice and opinions.

He glanced at the billboard in his rearview mirror. So why did her name come before his?

The worm comment was still bothering him when he walked into the station and marched into Amelia's office to complain about Jade's top billing. Maybe if he could get that changed ...

"Did you check your e-mail?" she asked without looking up from her laptop.

"What? No. Why?"

"Numbers came in late last night. I held on to them until this morning." She looked up at him. "They should be in your in-box now." Not a hint of anything—good or bad.

He didn't want to give her the satisfaction of looking at the numbers here. After that run-in with Barry, he wasn't sure he could handle seeing low numbers that showed he had a colossal climb before he topped the bastard.

Rome turned around and headed to his office. He could've sworn he heard Amelia laughing. The woman was a witch. Unless … His eyes widened. Maybe the numbers were good. Really good.

The mail app on his phone was open before he stepped into his office. *Big numbers. Big mother fu*—"Holy shit!" The numbers were huge—much bigger than he'd expected. So big he was officially back on top. *JADED … with Rome Rizzelli* was number one in the drive-time slot.

He jabbed a fist over his head, and then it dawned on him. Barry had seen these numbers last night like Amelia had. Running into Rome this morning must've been like rubbing rock salt in an open wound. He fist pumped again.

"Isn't it a little early for that sort of enthusiasm?"

Jade. Whatever wall he'd built between them crumbled as he turned and bum-rushed her, wrapping her up in his arms and spinning her around.

She squealed.

"We're number one!" he yelled. "The show is on top!"

"Oh my God!"

Around and around they went, until he veered into his desk and ended up half sitting, half standing with Jade between his legs. Her hands were on his shoulders. His hands were on her hips.

This is your chance to make things right, buddy. Take it. "I'm sorry I've been a jerk."

She nodded, but still, she stepped back beyond his reach. "Are you apologizing because you really mean it, or is that the numbers talking?"

"I really mean it. I was thinking about what to say to you even before the numbers came in."

She thought about it but simply nodded again. "Top of the charts. That's crazy."

No, what was crazy was the literal and figurative distance between them these past two weeks. He'd been such an idiot. He pushed off the desk and went to her. "Jade, you're right. We're good together."

Her face wrinkled. "But all good things come to an end, right?"

He reached for her hand and coaxed her closer. "Maybe. Probably. But they don't have to yet."

• • •

Jade wasn't sure how to respond as Rome brought her hand to his mouth and brushed her knuckles against his lips. Her insides went all wonky, even as one side of her brain said, "Don't listen to him," and the other side said, "Make him grovel."

Two minutes of adrenaline-induced niceties didn't erase two weeks of mostly cold shoulder.

"Let's celebrate tonight," he said, his fingers still laced with hers.

"Me too?" Amelia appeared in the doorway, looking suspicious.

A guilty heat spread over Jade's face as she snatched her hand away.

Rome only made it worse when he muttered, "Not the kind of celebrating I had in mind."

"Gotta get ready for the show." Jade rushed a requisite smile and then pushed past Amelia and out the door.

Four hours later, Jade figured the entire awkward scene was behind them, but Amelia cornered her near the coffeepot the minute the show was over and Rome had left the break room.

"Everything okay?" Amelia asked.

"Yeah. Why? Did the show sound bad?"

"Nope. In fact, the show was great. I'm talking about what I walked in on in Rome's office."

Jade played dumb.

"Sexual harassment is a big deal," Amelia said.

"Oh, no! It's not like that. Not at all." For crying out loud, Jade had started this whole ball rolling with one ill-advised kiss. "It's ... mutual."

Amelia nodded, but she didn't look any less concerned. Of course not.

Jade rushed to comfort her. "I know it's not cool for coworkers to ..." What where they now? Not a damn thing.

Amelia put up her hand. "I'm not really interested in your personal life. You and Rome have chemistry. That's clear. It's why you're so good on the air, but we're on top now, so we have a lot to lose. I just want to make sure we aren't building an empire on stilts. You know?"

Jade nodded and did her best to stand tall in the face of Amelia's scrutiny.

"Are you free for lunch?" Amelia asked.

It wasn't necessarily an odd question, but on the heels of the talk about Rome, it felt strange. Jade had never been very comfortable with face-to-face evasion, so she smiled and said, "I am."

"Good. I'm tired of eating alone." Amelia offered a weak laugh. "It would be nice to have another woman to commiserate with during my male-dominated day."

Jade laughed even while she remained unsettled by the entire conversation. Amelia had been good to her since the day they'd met. She'd championed for her and had given her a shot at something groundbreaking. Surely, Jade had time for one lunch.

She didn't have to talk about Rome.

But by the time Jade had finished her Caesar wrap, it was clear Amelia had a lot to say.

"He's charismatic. I'll give him that." Amelia took another big bite of her kale salad.

Jade nodded. She really didn't want to get dragged into a conversation like this.

"Normally, I'd put my foot down and just say no to a workplace romance. It's so much easier that way. But you two are a unique situation, and well, you got a jump start on me." She laughed at herself, but when the laughter faded, she stared right through Jade. "Maybe I'm crazy for wanting to run this station. Do you think I'm crazy?"

"No, I don't," Jade said, but if this lunch had taught her anything, it was that Amelia definitely needed someone to talk to. The woman had a lot on her mind.

"My dad left this place in a terrible mess, and radio's been all I've known since I was a kid. I cut my teeth on my father's knee *while* he was interviewing Bernie Kosar. I'm not kidding. I was chewing on my dad's knee." She smiled wistfully. "I can't let this station fail, but I refuse to make it soar the usual way. I don't care if sports radio doesn't traditionally talk about women's sports. I don't care if the female demographic is consistently ignored. Not by me. Not by my station. I'm going to do whatever I have to do to get what I want. Period. And I want a listener friendly, all-inclusive sports radio station, so I'm going for it."

"That's admirable." And enviable. To not only have the guts to do whatever it takes, but to know so clearly what you wanted in the first place.

"Listen, Jade, Rome's not a bad guy. I'd say he's a surly guy at best and maybe rightfully so. He's been putting up with me barking orders and giving him little wiggle room. I'm the bitch his nightmares are made of." The skin around her eyes crinkled playfully when she smiled, but then the happy expression faded. "Rome is better than he lets himself be. Do you know who Barry Vincent is?"

Jade nodded. She caught his show every once in a while. He was a lot like Rome, but more arrogant. He didn't even bother with callers half the time.

"Well, my dad hired Rome to cohost with Barry, and Barry didn't take kindly to the intrusion. He tried to screw things up for Rome every chance he got. He thought he could force the new kid out, but what actually ended up happening was my father gave Barry an ultimatum, deal with it or leave, and Barry left. That son of a bitch went off and got enough financing to start his own station. After that, Rome took over drive time and became the new Barry. Having you come in is probably giving him flashbacks." Amelia twitched like it was funny.

Was that what was going on? Still? Despite everything they'd shared, Rome really thought his job was threatened?

"I know he hates me," Amelia continued. "But every cult member hates his or her deprogrammer." She laughed.

Jade couldn't. Those were harsh words even if they, too, were meant to be funny. "Was the station really that bad when your father was here?"

"Bad enough that I fired the ones who wouldn't cooperate. I would've never fired Rome, though. I know all about his mother and sister, so I figure he could be coaxed into doing just about anything as long as it means he keeps his job. And I really do think he's starting to see I'm right." She raised her glass. "Here's to the number one morning show in Cleveland."

Jade raised her glass and offered a smile. This lunch had actually been enlightening. Apparently, Rome's standoffishness these last two weeks wasn't all about his ego. While she'd been completely honest about her not being a threat to his job, the station's history must've made it hard for him to believe her.

Maybe Rome would understand just how serious she was if she finally fessed up and told him just how serious she was about him.

She needed to talk to him and lay it all out on the line, once and for all.

•••

Rome didn't expect to see Jade again this afternoon. When she walked into his office sometime after 1:00 p.m., his mood spiked.

"Can I help you?"

She closed the door behind her, and every cell in his body jumped to the same hopeful conclusion. Celebration time? Maybe she'd thought about his apology and was ready to heartily accept it.

But she set her phone and keys on his desk, folded her hands, and leveled him with a depressingly serious look. "Can we talk?"

"About what?"

She cleared her throat before moving on. "About us."

Now, that could be a pleasant topic. He grinned. "What about us?"

"Well, I want an 'us.'"

He must not have been following her, because when he suggested she come on over and have a seat on his lap, she balked.

"No, thank you," she said. "I'm fine right here."

"But if you're there and I'm here, we aren't an 'us.'"

"Rome, be serious for a minute."

He made his most serious face. "How's that?"

She nodded her approval.

"I still think we could have this conversation with you on my lap."

That broke her the smallest bit, and she smiled, shaking her head until she stopped and stared at him with the goofiest expression. "I am not you, and you are not Barry Vincent."

She'd lost him. "Huh?"

"Amelia told me what happened when you were hired to be Barry's cohost. It got me thinking that maybe the wall between us these past couple weeks has been because you're afraid I'm going to consciously or unconsciously push you out somehow. I would never let that happen. Because ..." she hesitated. "I like you."

He took the flippant route because this was feeling a little heavy. "I like you, too."

"No, I really, really like you."

And that was exactly what he'd been afraid of. "Jade."

That one word changed the entire game. Her face fell even as her shoulders squared for battle. "I know this is the part where you tell me you don't do relationships. I don't either, but I was hoping ..."

He sat back in his chair and tipped his face to the ceiling as he exhaled. As God is his witness, he would've loved to have been in a position to take this chance with her.

"Listen." He looked at her again, doing his best not to let the seductive lift of her brow influence him. "You've seen what I'm up against. I own a ranch house and a minivan because I have two women who need me. They are always going to need me. Be honest with yourself. You don't want to be saddled with a man like that." It was harsh, but it was true.

"Well ..." She chewed on her bottom lip as she let that sink in, and as she did, her phone vibrated against his desk. Before she snatched it up, he saw the name of the caller: *Bon-Hwa.*

Even after what he'd just said, Rome felt that familiar, unentitled flare of possession. "He's still after you?"

Jade ignored the call, clutching the phone to her chest with both hands. "I don't care about him. I care about you."

And he couldn't help but see that as a problem. He could have a friend. He could have a lover. But he couldn't have a wife. How would that even work? In all of Rome's daydreams, he couldn't convince himself that a woman would ever fall for him hard enough to agree to a life that included living in the same small house as his mother and sister. It wasn't always pretty. Hell, there were days when even Rome, who loved them unconditionally, could barely manage the stress.

Jade deserved better. And maybe if he was out of the way, she could have it with somebody else—somebody who was even family approved like her neighbor's grandson.

He kept his face carefully neutral and ignored the dull ache in his chest. "I don't have a future to offer you. At least not the kind of future you deserve." He looked away from the disappointment on her face. "But, maybe he can."

"Are you serious?" She sounded pissed. "You're actually pushing me off on some other guy?"

He nodded. It was the absolute right thing to do.

Rome swiveled his chair around to the window as she slammed the door behind her. He couldn't watch her walk away without feeling like he'd made a terrible mistake.

Chapter Fifteen

They were flat. Again.

Rome felt the disconnect throughout the entire show. Four days ago, Jade had walked into his office wanting "an us," and he'd sent her away and the show mojo along with her. He had been worried about her needing him? *Try that the other way, buddy.* Especially when it came to the ratings.

There had to be some way to fix this. But those thoughts would have to wait, because Amelia walked in and sat in a chair facing his desk. "I don't get it. I would've thought you would've loved the idea of spending more time with her, but you're back to acting like it's the most painful four hours of your life."

He slapped his hands to his desk and glared at her, hoping she would stop.

She wasn't the least bit intimidated. "Please. I see the way you look at her." She made stupid puppy dog eyes.

"Leave, Amelia."

"I'll leave when I right this sinking ship." She smiled and grabbed a framed photo off his desk. "How's your mother?"

He snatched the picture back. "You don't give a shit about my mother."

"Don't be mean, Rome. I'm trying to be nice and break the ice here. You and I have been at each other's throats for months. I think it's time for a change. And since you don't want to talk about Jade, we're going to talk about your mother. How is your mother?" she asked again.

He threw his hands onto his head and exhaled loudly. "She's fine. She has a cold. I have to get out of here and pick up Luden's cherry cough drops and tissues with lotion, because her nose gets sore."

"How's your sister?"

He shook his head. "She's working, bagging groceries for people who are so fucking uncomfortable around a person with Down syndrome they pretend she isn't even there. Sounds like fun, huh?" About as much fun as this conversation. "Amelia, I don't have time for this."

"And I don't have the time to waste four prime hours of radio each morning." She stared at him. "You're talking over Jade. She can't find her voice. The jokes aren't funny. The callers are boring. And the numbers are down."

He groaned.

"What is going on?"

"I don't know." But he did. Apparently they couldn't be "an us" on air if they couldn't be "an us" off air.

"Are you in love with her?"

He laughed. "No."

"Of course not. Hard-assed Rome Rizzelli can't be bothered with something stupid like love. Am I right?" She unleashed that witchy grin. "You know, a few weeks ago, we had a full- blown romantic comedy full of sexual tension. Listeners were wondering will they or won't they? Are they or aren't they? It was amazing." She stared into space and nodded. "Who would've thought the magic formula for drive-time sports radio was romance?"

Unbelievable. He shook his head. "Men aren't listening to the show waiting for a love connection."

"You would be surprised." She looked at him again. "Nobody will be listening for long if you can't re-create the magic, though. Right now, all we have is you two spewing boring baseball facts. Boo! At this rate, I'd expect Barry Vincent to be back on top this time next week."

Rome grimaced. "That's not going to happen."

"I know it's not, because you're going to fix whatever is broken between you and Jade."

"That's exactly what I was just thinking about doing."

"Good. What's your plan?"

"I don't have one."

Amelia sighed. "Take her flowers. Apologize."

"I have nothing to apologize for. She's the one who wants something I can't give."

Amelia's brow raised. "What does she want?"

He was so out-of-sorts he actually answered. "A relationship."

Amelia laughed. "Is that all? I thought you were going to say something ridiculous like your job." Her eyes narrowed. "Why can't you give her a relationship, Rome? If you can leave your mother and sister long enough to do a four-hour radio show five days a week, you can give the woman a couple dates a month. Can't you?"

He rolled his eyes. "Is that what you call a relationship? A couple of dates a month?"

"Sure. Why? What do you call a relationship?"

"With me? I call it a dead end."

"Some of my favorite drives have been dead ends." She looked wistful, and again he thought she was crazy. "You know? You're overthinking this," she said.

Maybe, but it didn't matter. "Jade is involved with someone else." At least she should be.

"Interesting. So you're what? Doing the respectful thing, stepping aside and letting some other guy take the top spot? WHO ARE YOU?"

He was done with this conversation. He had cough drops to buy. "Whatever. Sure."

"Is that your plan for dealing with Barry Vincent, too?" She stood up and smoothed her skirt while his blood boiled. "You really have changed, Rome. I'm just not sure it's been altogether for the better."

He pounded his fists on his desk as she walked out of his office. "You're the devil! Do you know that?"

But when his echo died, he was left with one nagging thought: he may have changed, but not enough to give up the top spot. Maybe Amelia was right. Maybe it didn't have to be all or nothing.

And if that was the case, it was time to get back in the game.

• • •

Give the guy a chance.

If Jade had thought it once, she'd thought it a hundred times on this date. And now, she was faced with the question of whether or not to invite Bon-Hwa up to her apartment. For a nightcap. To talk. It didn't have to go farther than that. She didn't want it to go farther than that. *So don't invite him up.*

"I had a nice time," he said.

"Me too." Mostly. It wasn't earth-shattering or anything. But it was better than sitting home alone stewing about Rome.

She forced a smile and folded her hands in her lap as he pulled into her parking lot. *Ask him.* It was certainly what he wanted. Every time he looked at her, his eyes were filled with hope.

Fine. "Would you like to come up ... for a drink?" Maybe he would say no.

"Yes."

Give the guy a chance. She thought it all the way up the stairs while she avoided his hand every time it traveled her way. Maybe they just needed to talk more. Maybe the sparks would come.

When she opened the door and flipped on the light, she said, "I have beer, wine, and soda."

"I'll take a beer, please." So polite. He sat at the breakfast bar counter as she wandered over to the fridge, stealing a glance at him every now and then. Even his posture was perfect.

Maybe Rome had been right to push her into this. If she'd been willing to take a risk with a guy like him, didn't it stand to reason that it would be less of a risk with a guy like this?

She slid Bon-Hwa a beer and then twisted open her bottle of water. Now what? It wasn't like they could talk sports.

A knock on the door surprised and unsettled Jade until she figured it was probably just another random drop-in by Jillian, who'd forgotten her key.

"Expecting someone?" Bon-Hwa asked.

"No, but I bet it's my roommate. She's in and out, living mostly with her fiancé." Jade didn't bother looking through the peephole before she opened the door. "Did you lose your ..."

Rome stood in the hallway with a bouquet of roses and a wavering smile. "Hey."

"Hey."

He glanced behind her into the kitchen, and that was all it took. His features hardened for a second before his face went blank. "I found these on your mat." He handed the flowers to her. "Have a good night."

"What?" She looked at the flowers and then back and Rome, who was trucking it down the hall.

"I thought you just worked together," Bon-Hwa said.

"We do." She shook her head. "But it's complicated."

He snorted. "Then maybe I should leave."

"No." The last thing she needed was him going back to his grandmother and telling her about this. "I'm sure it's just some office prank."

Bon-Hwa didn't look like he was buying it.

Neither was she. What was Rome Rizzelli up to now?

•••

Screw the games. Rome couldn't play them anymore. He absolutely couldn't let Amelia keep pulling his strings. That led to ridiculous things like barging in on Jade's date and looking like a complete fool. No more. He'd had his fill.

It was time to figure out Plan B. Everybody had a plan B. And with the way things were going at the station, he had a feeling he was going to need his sooner rather than later.

He'd always thought writing snarky op-ed pieces for newspapers and magazines would be cool. Yeah, that would work. Plan freaking B. Although, did anyone read newspapers and magazines anymore? Some people did, but probably not enough to make it a lucrative career. He could always scout online news outlets. That would work. In fact, he would probably need assignments from all over to make a living as a freelance sports writer.

The word freelance made him shudder. Waiting on paychecks wouldn't be fun.

He glanced in the rearview mirror and caught sight of his eyes. They were shadowed in darkness, and his pupils were dull. Vacant. He tipped the mirror toward him. Jesus, he was a mess. He needed to shave. He needed to sleep. He needed to stop wondering if there would ever be a way to give Jade what she wanted.

His phone rang, and he half expected, half hoped it was Jade calling to talk about what had happened tonight. But it was an unknown caller, and he ignored it. He wasn't in the mood to talk to anybody really. But several seconds later, he was intrigued by the message notification.

He pressed the phone to his ear and listened to the familiar voice with about as much enthusiasm as he listened to shrill audio feedback at a remote show.

"Rome, it's Barry. Remember when I told you not to get too comfortable?" The asshole chuckled. "Well, it's time to shake things up. Do something nobody ever expected. Call me when you have time to talk. I mean it. Call me. Don't be a dick because you think I'm a dick. It's time to get over ourselves, and I have just the thing. Would you be interested in a new home for *Riled Up with Rome*?" He chuckled again. "I'm dead serious. Call me if it's still in ya, man."

What the hell? Rome dropped the phone on the passenger seat and stared at the merging traffic. Was Barry Vincent going to offer him a job?

Would you be interested in a new home for Riled Up with Rome? Barry Vincent's radio station wanted to lure Rome away from the competition? Any other day, Rome would've laughed in the guy's face. But not tonight—tonight, he was feeling sort of vulnerable. Besides, *if* Barry had a home for *Riled Up with Rome*, maybe that could be his Plan B.

Rome glanced at the phone. The thought of calling the guy who'd tried to push him out of WKST ten years ago left a bad taste in his mouth. Or maybe the bad taste came from hitting rock bottom after Amelia London's puppet strings had finally snapped.

It couldn't hurt to listen to Barry.

Chapter Sixteen

"I have a plan."

Jade looked up to find Amelia pouring herself a cup of coffee.

"We're going to go back to the Man vs. Woman remotes. Rome's shoulder has to be better by now. Honestly, I think he was just milking it."

"It was his pec," Jade said. "He tore it. That's a painful injury. He wasn't milking anything."

Amelia frowned. "Don't make excuses for him. I don't want you in his corner. It makes for bad radio." She snapped the lid onto her travel mug. "I can help with that. Next week we're doing the show from The Skating Club. Man vs. Woman: Deep Freeze." She grinned like the idea was brilliant.

"I can't ice skate," Jade said.

"I know. I remembered you saying that back when we were brainstorming MvW options." She raised her cup to her lips, but didn't drink. "Rome was a first-team hockey all-star in high school. Did you know that?"

Jade shook her head. "Doesn't seem like much of a competition."

"Nope, and if he humiliates you, then maybe you'll get some of your bite back." She smiled. "If you're not going to be making goo-goo eyes at him, then I need to see your fangs."

A shadow moved past the door. Had it been any faster, she wouldn't have recognized him.

"Rizzelli, get in here!" Amelia strummed her fingers on her travel mug and waited.

Jade's stomach rolled. They still hadn't discussed what the deal was with those flowers. She wasn't sure she wanted to anyway. She definitely refused to get her hopes up again. He already knew what she thought and where she was coming from. If he couldn't do any better than shove a bouquet of flowers at her without even taking proper credit for it, then nothing had changed.

"Rizzelli!" Amelia yelled again.

He seemed to appear out of nowhere. "What?" He didn't sound like he was in the mood to mess around.

"Next week, we're bringing back Man vs. Woman."

"No, we're not," he said.

One of Amelia's pencil-thin brows arched. "Really? Well, my master schedule says otherwise."

He glanced at Jade, and something almost agonizing passed across his face before he looked back at Amelia and shook his head. "I was going to save this until we had some privacy, but it is what it is ... I quit."

Jade gasped.

Coffee sputtered on Amelia's lips. "Not funny."

"Not trying to be. I'm serious. I met with Barry Vincent. He's offered me a time slot,"

Amelia's eyes bugged out. "You can't leave. Your contract is iron-clad. There's a noncompete clause."

"Barry's legal eagles are looking for a way out right now."

"Yeah? Well, I have legal eagles, too." Amelia bolted from the room.

For a minute, Jade thought Rome was going to walk out without saying another word, but then he stopped and turned.

"*This* is where it ends," he said.

But why? She knew how much this job meant to him. She knew how much he hated Barry Vincent. Why was he going to such extremes?

"Rome, think about this. Please. It doesn't have to be this way. What if you're making a terrible mistake?"

He nodded, but he didn't look at her. "I have thought about it. A lot actually. And this is the only way it can be."

"Why? Explain it to me. Does this have anything to do with the flowers?"

He looked pained. "That never should've happened. I'm sorry." He started to walk away.

"Rome, I'll quit. I'll go back to teaching, and you can stay."

That slowed his steps, and when he turned, he offered her a sad smile. "You want to be here, Jade. Admit it. And you deserve to be here. God knows Amelia wants you around more than she wants me. So stay. I'll go. The way I look at it, walking out on my own terms is better than being fired trying to meet hers."

"But Amelia would never fire you. She told me that at lunch the other day."

He didn't look convinced. "The deed is done. I said the words. Now, it's time to face the consequences." He seemed to think about it a little more with a furrowed brow, and then he simply ended with, "I'll be okay."

So would she. No doubt about it. She'd been through much worse.

But still, this hurt a lot more than she'd expected it to.

• • •

"Why are you home?" Tess asked.

Because I'm an idiot. Rome tossed his keys into the bowl by the door and figured he better look into draining his retirement account, because that's exactly what this might come to if Barry didn't pull through with the job.

Nothing like relying on a sworn enemy.

"I quit," he said.

Tess looked moderately concerned. "Are you sad? Don't be sad. The store is hiring. You can work with me."

He set aside his own worries for a minute and looked at how happy the idea of him bagging groceries made her. "I don't know," he said. "We'd probably get in too much trouble, don't you think?" He grabbed an orange off the counter and tossed it to her. She bobbled it, but she made the catch, laughing. "Can we do that with the produce?"

"No way!"

"That's what I thought." He caught the orange when she sent it sailing back, and then he returned it to the bowl. "But don't worry. I've got another job in radio lined up, Tess. I'm just not sure when it will start. This is sort of like a vacation." With a lot more stress.

"Oh, that's not so bad. We can do puzzles together until you start."

"You bet we can."

Somewhere in the distance, he heard the telltale tune of his lead-in music, and his brow furrowed. Maybe he was hearing things. "Are you listening to my show, Tess?"

She nodded. "I always do ... until Aunt Karen gets Mom dressed and they come out at seven to watch *Good Morning America*."

"That's probably not a good idea anymore. Not until I ..." He froze at the sound of Jade's voice.

"Hey, folks. Welcome to Jaded ..." She seemed to stumble over the word and then forget the rest.

"With Rome Rizzelli," he added under his breath.

Tess laughed.

"I'm your host Jade Wren, and we've got lots to talk about today. Lots of headlines."

Would she address his absence? He moved closer to the radio.

She seemed to stumble again, but before he could conjecture why, she steamrolled right into the show they had planned *together*.

"For starters, the White Sox are in town, and rumor has it, they don't respect our pitching staff. Jerry Rolland, who was ejected from last night's game after a heated exchange with the home plate umpire, is on record as saying All-Star Brent Brumbaugh is—and I quote—'a big baby, who won't hit back.' Ouch! That seems harsh. But I don't know. Maybe it's true, because I haven't seen Brumbaugh or any of our guys defend their batters by hitting a single opponent in return. What do you think? If your star outfielder gets pegged on average once every series, and your pitching staff doesn't retaliate, are you weak? Are you being walked on? Are you rolling over and letting your biggest divisional rival rub your proverbial tummy? Talk to me."

She rattled off the station's phone number, sounding good. Strong. As if nothing unusual had gone down that morning. Maybe she'd already forgotten him.

He had the sudden urge to remind her.

"Tess, where's your phone?"

"Charging beside my bed. Why?"

"I need to borrow it."

He didn't know who the station's gatekeeper was today, but he wouldn't put it past Amelia to have his cell phone number on a sticky note below the words DO NOT ACCEPT CALLERS FROM THIS NUMBER. She was going to have to do better than that if she wanted to keep him out.

He may have quit, but right now, he didn't feel like going quietly.

"Rome, what are you doing home?" Aunt Karen, whose shift started after he'd left in the morning and ended before he got home, stood at the end of the hall with an armful of laundry, looking surprised to see him.

"Long story. I'll fill you in later." He ducked into the closest room, Tess's room, and closed the door.

This was rock bottom, wasn't it? Locked in his sister's room, surrounded by posters of ponies and One Direction while he dialed up the radio station he'd just left, so he could harass his replacement.

You were the one who quit.

He almost hung up before the call was answered. Almost. But then an unfamiliar voice said, "Thanks for calling Sports Radio 94.7. Who would you like to talk to, and what is the topic you are calling about?"

Here goes nothing. Rome cleared his throat and did his best to disguise his voice. "Lemme talk to Jade about Brumbaugh."

"And you are?"

"Lamar."

He saw himself in the mirror on the back of Tess's door and tossed a pillow in the direction of his judgmental reflection.

The next thing he knew, Jade's voice was in his ear as the show played over the line while he was on hold. "I'm not saying whether it's right or wrong."

And that was a problem. "Pick a side and go with it," he wanted to say. He'd taught her better than that. But he was stuck in the queue, and she wouldn't hear him. Besides, he probably shouldn't be helping the competition. Why the hell was he calling? *To talk to her.*

He needed to get that out of his system. Mooning over Jade wasn't going to help him sharpen his tongue in time to go back to hosting *Riled Up with Rome.*

"Hitting someone on purpose doesn't show good sportsmanship," a female caller said.

Whether he could be heard or not, he countered with his patented, acerbic reply, "Ever heard of football? How 'bout hockey? Those guys hit the shit out of each other in a display of good sportsmanship. You moron." See? He could do this. It was still in him.

But in a flash of ancient memory, he remembered being a teenager beating the crap out of a neighbor kid who'd called Tess the same thing. *Moron.* The memory made him wince, and he wondered if Tess had heard him just now. Even worse, how long had she been listening to his show? Before Jade? He'd said some terrible things back then.

He should've been more careful. Going forward, he was going to have to forbid her from listening to the *Riled Up with Rome* reboot. The trouble was that just sat like all sorts of wrong in his gut.

"Hey, Lamar. You're on the air with Jade. What are your thoughts on Brumbaugh? Lamar?"

Crap. Lamar. That was him. But his heart wasn't in it anymore.

Rome started to take the phone away from his ear so he could hang up when he heard Jade's voice again. "Lamar, are you there?"

God, he just wanted to talk to her even though he was pretty sure she would hang up on him.

He lowered his voice and tried on a battered and bruised Cockney accent leftover from high school drama class. "Brumbaugh ain't nothin' but a li'l girl. He might wanna grow a pair 'fore he takes the field again. Hittin' batters is part of the game. Ya can't play the game right, then go play softball." He didn't get a single shred of satisfaction out of it.

The line was so quiet for a minute he thought he'd been detected and disconnected, but then he heard a muffled, dry laugh. "Interesting perspective, Lamar." Jade hit the name hard and drew it out long.

Yep. She was laughing. At him. And it was one part amusement—probably over his ridiculously terrible accent—and one part condescension that after he'd quit, he was back to badgering her. *Busted, Rizzelli.* He deserved to be cut off completely.

"Here's the thing, *Lamar*. My best friend in high school played softball, and her philosophy toward any batter who crowded the plate was to peg her. Hard. She broke ribs. You do that once; you make room in the strike zone." Jade's soft chuckle filtered over the line, making him feel like he was beside her once again. "Alaina didn't have any problem hitting a batter, so I guess that blows your theory about little girls and softball. The bottom line ... once again ... gender has nothing to do with any of this, *Lamar*."

He grinned. She was sharp, rocking the mic and getting in jabs. He'd taught her well.

"Don't call back until you grow up and get a clue." The line clicked as she hung up.

Maybe he'd taught her a little too well.

●●●

Jade watched in silence as Amelia wore a path in the carpet outside the studio where they'd just endured their first Rome-less show.

"How pathetic! He quits, and then the first thing he does is call into the show he abandoned. I should've fired him months ago. We don't need him." Amelia's normally coiffed hair frizzed out on all sides. "You're my ace, now. We'll simply roll with it. Three months, and I'll have a solo woman on top of the sports radio charts. What do you think of that?"

"It sounds great." It also sounded like something that would take more than three months, but she wasn't going to say anything to get Amelia any more fired up.

"It'll be awesome, but I need to get marketing behind us. Quick."

Amelia power walked down the hall toward her office, phone pressed to her ear.

Jade just stood there processing everything that had happened in the last six hours. Rome had quit. Jade had gone solo. And Rome had called in to badger her live on the air. She didn't know which part was most ridiculous. She didn't know what really and truly came next.

But as she walked down the hallway toward her office and past his, a little pang of sadness sparked in her chest. He'd marched himself right into the throes of a self-fulfilling prophecy. And somehow, that changed the way she looked at things here. The dream had gone sour, and she wasn't sure there was a way to fix it.

A few steps farther down the hall, Jade's phone vibrated in her hand, and Laurel Moses's name flashed on the screen. What was the principal of Sunrise Academy doing calling her? She hadn't talked to anyone there except human resources since the day she'd been laid off. Her first thought was, what if something had gone wrong with her unemployment? She'd heard of people having to payback thousands after they'd started working again.

That was all she needed.

But when she took a breath and answered the call, she was surprised to find Laurel sounding downright happy.

"I have great news!" Laurel said. "The school has been gifted some money, which has allowed us to rework the budget. How would you like your old job back?"

Jade walked into the break room and dropped onto the nearest chair. Was this a joke? Of all days. Seriously, if there was any doubt in her mind about staying at this station, Laurel Moses had just given her the easy way out.

Chapter Seventeen

Rome finished cutting the back half of the grass and pulled the earbuds from his ears. Another hour spent listening and talking to Jade when in reality he was just talking to himself. If Barry didn't get back to him soon, he would be certifiably insane.

Tess bolted out of the house. "Aunt Karen brought me a new puzzle. You wanna do the edges?"

What was Aunt Karen doing here? He'd told her to take some time off while he was unemployed.

"I'd love to, kiddo. Just let me put the mower away and wash up."

After a quick rinse of his hands in the bathroom sink, he headed down the hall to the living room, where his mother was in her lounge chair with the television on mute so she could talk to her sister. Puzzle pieces were scattered on a folding table in the corner, and that was where Tess sat. The biggest smile was on her face.

"Puppies," she said, holding up the cardboard cover.

"Excellent." That kid could make him enjoy anything. "Aunt Karen, I didn't expect to see you." He placed a quick kiss on her cheek. "You're supposed to be on vacation. I figured you and Uncle Nate would be halfway to the beach by now." He laughed even as she made a face.

"Nate didn't want to go. He didn't *feel* like it. So I didn't feel like hanging around the house with him."

Rome wasn't exactly surprised. In the five years Aunt Karen had been married to her third husband, Nate, she'd complained about him more than she'd ever complimented him.

"That stinks," he said.

His mother pointed toward the other side of the room. "Rome, there's a message for you."

His heartbeat stuttered. "What kind of message?"

"A phone message. Some guy named Barry called the house."

What? "When?" He'd been waiting days for that call.

He scrambled toward the antiquated answering machine and pressed play. "Why would he call here?"

"Because you live here?" his mother smarted back.

Yeah, but who called landlines anymore? "Rome, it's Barry. Call me back when you have a chance."

An even mix of hope and dread lay heavy like a ball of knots in his chest.

"Tess, the puzzle's going to have to wait just a sec." He hightailed it back to his room and dialed Barry's cell number.

It rang and rang so long Rome thought he might have to leave a message.

"Barry Vincent."

"Barry, it's Rome, returning your call."

In the few beats of silence before Barry spoke, the dread won out, and then Rome knew why.

"Deal's off," Barry said.

Just like that.

"Even if we were able to pay the ridiculous amount they want to release you from the noncompete, which we aren't, they would retain the name of the show. *Riled Up with Rome* belongs to WKST with or without you. So it's a no go."

"Damn it." Rome should've seen this coming.

"I wish I had better news—for you. It's all good for me, considering ratings are out and your old show is tanking hard. Guess who's back on top again?" He laughed.

Rome closed his eyes and swallowed hard. "You played me. Didn't you, Barry?"

"Now, now, Rome. You're the one who quit before you had a signed contract in your hands. You've got nobody to blame but your ego and your mouth." The worst thing about it was Barry wasn't wrong. Maybe that's why Rome didn't feel like arguing.

He sat on the end of his bed and let the phone drop to the floor. Now what? Crawling back to Amelia was not an option—even though Jade had claimed Amelia would've never fired him in the first place. He'd been such a jerk about a lot of things, he didn't deserve the second chance anyway. Maybe what he needed was a clean slate, somewhere where Rome Rizzelli's reputation wouldn't precede him. Maybe he should follow Glenn. But how could he take Mom and Tess away from Cleveland?

He heard rustling outside his door, and despite the gravity of the situation, he smiled. "Tess, you can come in. I'm off the phone."

She opened the door. "Can we do the puzzle then?"

He had a much bigger puzzle he needed to solve, but once again, he couldn't stand to disappoint her. "Absolutely. Bring on the puppies."

She whooped, and for a split second, all the happiness he'd felt that day at the football game roared in.

"Hey, Tess. Do you ever think about leaving Cleveland?"

She looked at him like he was crazy. "No. Why?"

"No reason." None that he wanted to bother her with now, anyway.

• • •

"I'm sorry. I thought I heard you say you're quitting to go back to teaching."

Jade bristled at Amelia's harsh tone. "That's what I said."

Amelia poked a finger at the ceiling and said, "If this your idea of making me miss you, ha! I don't. You were a sucky father and an even suckier station owner. You got me into this mess, and I will get myself out."

Great. Jade had gone and pushed her boss off the edge into insanity. "I'm sorry, Amelia. It's just that ... I'm a teacher."

"Don't give me that bull crap. You're nothing but a pushover. You take the easy road—except on the football field because it's okay for you to push people around there."

Jade smacked a hand to her chest like she'd been hit. But as she sat there weathering Amelia's glares, she knew there was some truth in it.

"Tell me really why you would give up the opportunity to have a stereotype-breaking career, doing something that makes you happy. Or at least it made you happy until ..." Amelia's eyes widened. "This isn't about teaching. This is about Rome."

"It's not." But it sort of was.

"Oh, for crying out loud! You're in love with the selfish jerk. Be honest with yourself." Amelia shook her head. "I'm sorry he turned out to be such an asshole, but newsflash—he's a guy. Guys are idiots. It's a universal truth. I can only imagine what a line of bull he gave you the night he tried to fix things."

Jade blinked a few times. "What do you know about that night?" Jade hadn't said a word about that night to anyone but the two men who had been there and her closest friends.

Amelia fidgeted. "It's not really a big deal. On second thought, yes, it is a big deal. Or at least, it was a big deal. The show was falling apart, and I had to do something. Since I knew you two had this thing going ..." she waved her hands back and forth, "when things soured, I told him he needed to go fix whatever was broken in order to save the damn show, or he could kiss the top spot goodbye. He was supposed to take you flowers and apologize. His apology must've been horrible. I should've figured as much. The guy can't get a point across unless he's insulting someone."

So *that* had been the deal with the roses. She waited for it to settle one way or the other. It just sort of sat there in no man's land. Knowing the catalyst for the odd encounter didn't really change anything, except maybe it highlighted how pushy Amelia could be. The thing was, Rome could be pushy, too. He just never seemed to be pushy in the right direction.

Jade exhaled. "I admire you for what you're trying to do here. I really do, but it's all gone sour for me. I don't know what else to say." She stood. "I won't leave you high and dry like Rome did. I'll keep doing the show until the end of the month. That's when school starts. Hopefully you can find someone by then."

"How generous of you," Amelia said wryly.

"I really am sorry."

"Me, too. You're good, Jade. It's just a shame you're letting other people dictate how good."

As she left Amelia's office, Jade told herself not to be wounded by the harsh words. Amelia was angry and rightfully so. Jade could see her boss's side of the argument, too. But the more she thought about Amelia's parting shot, the more she saw something else.

The woman had just made the biggest point of all.

...

New Jersey.

Rome rested his cheek on his fist and stared through the e-mail from the station manager at WKRZ in Trenton, where his former producer Glenn had landed. How was he supposed to take this seriously? Then again, how could he not? It was his only viable offer. And it was a good one. Cohosting a sports talk morning show with Kyle Cloker, who was every bit as salty as Rome had been, seemed like the perfect professional fit.

He focused on one particular sentence in the e-mail: *We make the FCC work to earn their fines.* Man, talk about the direct opposite of working for and with Amelia London. Nobody at WKRZ was going to slap him on the hand if he humiliated callers. Nobody was going to ream him out for sounding the emergency broadcasting signal and costing the station a few grand. That kind of behavior would be welcomed and expected. He'd be back to throwing barbs and not giving a shit where they landed in no time. In short, it was heaven.

Or it would be, if it weren't for that nagging ache in his chest and a soul-sucking lack of enthusiasm.

He shut his laptop and left his bedroom. Now was as good a time as any to bounce this off his family. The retirement funds were dwindling fast.

Aunt Karen, who still hadn't taken him up on the offer to take a real vacation, was at the kitchen sink, rinsing vegetables. A line of pill bottles on the window ledge cast a shadow on her face, and she was humming—despite all the trouble he knew she was having with Nate. It was downright crazy how happiness found a way.

"Tess, get me a Coke." His mother didn't even bother to look away from the television.

"Okay," Tess said. She didn't even bother to look up from her puzzle.

What a piece of work. He'd given his mother a Coke earlier in the day. And according to her doctor, that was more than enough caffeine for a twenty-four-hour period. His mother knew that. She was just trying to game the system.

"No more Coke," he said, startling them both.

His mother looked guilty. Tess looked reprimanded. So Rome laughed to let them know they were both off the hook.

"Aunt Karen, can you come in here for a minute?" he asked. "I want to talk to you guys about something. I need some advice."

She walked in, wiping her hands on a dishtowel, a curious expression on her face. "Everything okay?"

"Oh, he's going to tattle on me, because he gave me a Coke this morning." His mother pouted.

"No, I wasn't, but you just came clean, so thank you."

Tess giggled.

He hoped she was still able to at least smile after she heard this news.

"I've been offered a job in Trenton, New Jersey," he said.

His mother didn't seem impressed. "So what? It's not like you can take it."

"Mom, it's getting harder and harder to think something else will come up. I have to at least consider taking it."

"Are you moving?" Tess asked.

"Not just me. If I move, we all move."

Tess shook her head. "New Jersey is far away."

"Yes, it is."

His mother scoffed. "I'm not going anywhere. My doctors are here."

"My job is here," Tess said. "Aunt Karen is here."

He powered through the raw emotions rising in his chest. "I know, but New Jersey has doctors and grocery stores. We'll find everything we need there."

"I'm not going," his mother said.

"Me neither," Tess said.

He sighed. This was as bad as he'd expected it to be. "Can we just talk about this a little more before completely trashing it? Please? I can't keep hanging around at home with no money coming in. I need to figure out what comes next, and I need you both to understand that if the only option is outside of Cleveland, it won't be easy, but we'll be fine."

Aunt Karen cleared her throat. "What if there was another option?" She walked up behind his mother's chair. "I've been wanting to talk to you about something, but then you lost your job, and I didn't want to pile on more." She took a breath. "Nate and I are getting a divorce."

"I'm sorry to hear that," he said.

Aunt Karen waved off his concern. "I was thinking about moving in here with you."

Talk about timing. Especially if she was willing to move to New Jersey, too? Mom and Tess might get on board easier, and he would have some peace of mind knowing his mother and sister were being cared for by someone familiar, someone he trusted, while he was at work.

"What would you think about moving to New Jersey?" he asked.

Aunt Karen shook her head. "I'm not necessarily opposed, but what if you move to New Jersey, and the three of us stay here?"

It was a novel idea. Maybe too novel. "I don't know how that would work. I can't afford to support two households."

"You wouldn't have to pay me anymore, and I'll be getting alimony from Nate. Besides, I knew this divorce was coming so I stashed away some cash to help when I was on my own. Between that and the Social Security and disability funds, we should be pretty close to covering the major things here. Certainly, you could afford a one-bedroom in New Jersey."

That was ... crazy, wasn't it? The idea of Aunt Karen taking charge 24-7 while he was hundreds of miles away? What would he do with the downtime? A big blank space hung in his head.

"Don't you ever think about having a family of your own?" Aunt Karen asked. "A wife? Kids? You know, happily ever after?"

"Yeah, with Jade," Tess said.

He'd chuckled through every one of Aunt Karen's questions, but when Tess chimed in, that damn ache in his chest grabbed hold and stole his breath. "Not really," he said. "I never really saw myself as the marrying kind."

"Well, maybe it's time you started seeing yourself differently," his mother said.

He stared at her, and for the first time in a long time, he saw the possibilities.

"I think it's a good idea, Rome," his mother said. "We'll be just fine, the three of us. We'll have more fun without you, too."

"You're still only getting one Coke a day, Bea," Aunt Karen said.

Tess giggled, but then she frowned. "I would miss you."

It killed him. "I would miss you, too, kiddo." In fact, he wasn't sure he wanted to be away from her any longer than the four hours he'd spent at the station five days a week and the handful of hours a month he'd spent at remote broadcasts. He'd never been big on going out and getting away. He certainly didn't like the idea of being so far away he couldn't get to her in a matter of minutes.

Again he wondered how he would fill his days. Entire weekends to himself? That would be ridiculous.

Almost immediately, his brain started conjuring up images of fishing trips, endless football on TV, and lazy afternoons in bed ... with Jade.

He really wished Tess hadn't mentioned her name.

"You can visit him." Aunt Karen said. "We all will. We'll take a road trip. Which means you'll have to give physical therapy a real shot, lady." She tapped her sister on the shoulder.

Rome's mother didn't balk.

Were they really having this conversation? Was this really a possibility? He roughed a hand over his mouth and sucked in a big breath to stabilize his racing heart. "I'm not saying I've agreed to this plan, but *if* I did, I would come back to visit you, too."

"A lot?" Tess asked.

"A lot."

He was crazy for even thinking it was an option, wasn't he? Even if he could get past leaving his mother and sister in Ohio, would he even want a life like that?

Not really. New Jersey was a Plan B, at best. But Aunt Karen moving in, and him moving out, that could be his new Plan A.

More thoughts. Jade fighting her way across the goal line. Jade flush against the living room wall. Jade smiling at him over her laptop screen. Jade standing in his office at WKST.

I don't have a future to offer you. At least not the kind of future you deserve.

But now maybe he did. And if he played his cards right, it didn't have to have anything to do with New Jersey.

Chapter Eighteen

Jade dropped the bar stacked with 100 pounds of free weights to the mat with a clang. "Do I let other people determine how good I am?"

Jillian stopped mid stomach crunch on the incline bench. "Are you going to hit me if I say, 'maybe'?"

"Why's she gonna hit you?" Tanya asked as she walked up, unwinding her hand wraps after a go at MJ in the ring.

"I'm not going to hit anybody. I'm just looking for some perspective."

"Perspective on what?" MJ asked, and then she guzzled water until the plastic bottle crackled.

"Amelia said it's a shame I let other people determine how good I am. I honestly thought I'd moved past that. I mean I moved out of my mother's house. I took a job in radio. I took risks when it came to Rome." She'd been prepared to take those risks even farther. "I won a championship. Well, *we* won a championship." She smiled. "And a week ago, I lifted another personal best. What am I missing that Amelia is seeing?"

Jillian swung around until her knees were bent and her feet were on the floor at the bottom of the bench. "Are you happy to go back to teaching?"

Jade shrugged. "I'm happy to get away from the mess at the studio."

"That's not what she asked," Tanya said.

Jade took a second to think. "Yeah, I'm happy about teaching." But mostly she was indifferent.

"Could've fooled me," Jillian said. "Girl, what do you *really* want? What makes your heart sing?"

MJ set her water bottle on the end of the bench. "Let's do it this way. Where do you see yourself in five years?"

In five years, she would be thirty-one. And there were certain things a thirty-one-year-old should have achieved. "If I don't get hit by budget cuts again, I'll probably be teaching at Sunrise Academy. And if Umma and Halmoni get their way, I'll probably be married. Maybe even pregnant." That seemed like such a stretch.

"Both of those things are dependent on what someone else wants," MJ said.

They were, weren't they?

"What about the rest? What about football?" Tanya asked. "What will football look like in five years?"

Jade was still rattled by MJ's statement. "Um, maybe I can be a volunteer coach."

Tanya gasped. "Why wouldn't you play?"

"I don't know. I guess I figured it's kind of hard to play when you're pregnant, and thirty-one is kind of old for football."

"Girl, shut your mouth!" Tanya made a face. "They're going to have to drag my wrinkled-up, old ass off that field."

"I don't know," Jade said. "I don't do well with hypotheticals."

Jillian moved closer. "Hypothetical or not, your five-year plan sucks. Boring job. Nice guy. Kids." She gave an exaggerated shudder. "Sounds like the kind of five-year plan a mother wishes on her daughter just so she can stop worrying about her little girl's safety and get her hands on some grandkids." Jillian gave Jade a knowing look.

That was true. "So my five-year plan is uninspired. I'll work on it."

"You do that," MJ said. "Just make sure it's *your* plan."

"And make sure it includes you actually playing football," Tanya added.

Jade smiled. "Okay. Let's try this again. In five years, I see myself ..." The same uninspired future formed in her head. *Come on, Jade. What would you choose?* "Playing football. In fact, I see us with at least two more title wins." She grinned when her friends whooped their approval. "I see myself ..." Teaching? Was that really what *she* wanted to do? The only other job experience she had was on the radio, and she'd loved that. Well, she'd loved it up until Rome left. Okay, she hadn't always loved it even when Rome was around. *Because you let other people decide how great you should be.* Amelia had been absolutely right about that. What if she approached her entire life like she approached football and weight lifting? Determined to be great.

"I see myself on the radio," she said emphatically. "Top of the ratings." Regardless of who or what was messing up around her.

Still, she wished for one particular person to be messing up beside her.

"What about Rome?" Jillian asked.

"Are you psychic or something?"

MJ laughed. "No. You mouthed his name."

Jade slapped her forehead. "I'm losing my mind."

"Nah, just your inhibitions." Tanya gave Jade's arm a playful jab. "And that's a good thing. Is Rome in your five-year plan?"

"He didn't want to be in my one-year plan, let alone five." She frowned. And yet ... "Out of the blue, he texted me the other day."

"Girl, you didn't tell us that!" Tanya's eyes bugged out. "What did he say?"

"Not much. It was just small talk."

Jillian gasped. "He was fishing."

"Fishing for what?"

MJ shook her head. "For you! Trying to see if you were still interested enough and available to talk to him."

Jade thought about that for a second. "No. I think you're wrong. He has no reason to. The man made it clear. He doesn't do relationships."

"You don't do relationships, either," Jillian said laughing.

"None of us did." MJ flashed her wedding ring. "It happens."

More laughter, and when it died, Tanya spoke up. "Text him. Tell him you've been thinking about him. See where that leads."

"And who knows," Jillian said. "Maybe somehow, some way, it will last."

Jade guessed that sounded reasonable—just a quick text to check on him and let him know she was thinking about him. She'd done it before. It wasn't that much of a stretch. No, the bigger stretch was figuring out what to say to Amelia to get her job back ... and the biggest stretch of all was getting Umma and Halmoni on board with all of it.

• • •

"What will you do if you don't go back to teaching?" Umma's face wrinkled with concern, making her look instantly older.

Maybe Jade dropping all of this at once on them was selfish. Probably. But holding it in had become too self-destructive. Making other people happy was good, but that didn't mean making herself happy was bad. She could do this. She *had* to do this, so she could move on once and for all and be the complete woman she knew she could be.

"I'm going to talk to Amelia about keeping my job at the station, and if that doesn't work out, then I'll go back to school and study broadcasting, so I can get another job in radio or television someday."

"Back to school?" Umma's face paled.

"You won't have to pay a penny of the tuition. I'll take care of everything. It's my decision. It's my responsibility."

Halmoni shook her head. "Why would you want to start all over?"

"Because I want to do what makes me happy."

"Teaching doesn't make you happy?" Her mother looked wounded.

Jade weathered a wave of guilt, but it wasn't nearly as strong as it had been. "Talking about sports makes me happier."

Umma and Halmoni shared a glance. A few agonizing seconds later, Umma reached across the table for Jade's hand. "All we ever wanted is for you to be happy. So you go talk to Amelia. You will always have teaching to fall back on."

Not this time, Jade was done playing it safe. Now, it was all or nothing. Her mother and grandmother were going to have to get used to seeing every part of her—even the part that made decisions that would scare them.

She patted her mother's hand. "I won't need teaching to fall back on, because I'm not going to fail in radio." She smiled. "And there's more."

Halmoni sat ramrod straight like she was already on the defensive. Umma let go of Jade's hand, the concern returning to her face.

Maybe there was reason to worry. A job change seemed a lot less risky than trying to have some semblance of a relationship with Rome. Even if they ever got that far, would her mother and grandmother ever be able to judge him on his merits alone? Or would he always walk in the shadow of her father.

Jade exhaled. She wanted them all to break free. Maybe this was the only way.

"I met someone," Jade said. "Actually, you've met him, too."

For a minute, her mother and grandmother looked hopeful.

"I knew you would go back to Bon-Hwa," Umma said.

"It's not Bon-Hwa. It's Rome."

"The American," her grandmother said, clearly disappointed.

"He's short," her mother said, no happier.

"Yep. He's also occasionally rude and often misguided, but I can work with that." Jade reached for their hands. "Don't be scared. Even though it may seem like it sometimes, he's really nothing like Dad."

"How do you know?" Halmoni asked.

"Because despite all those things I just said, he's a genuinely good guy. You met his sister. He takes care of her and his mother, who's disabled. He puts his family first." And that was something her father had never done.

Umma's face softened, but she still wasn't convinced. "You should try again with Bon-Hwa."

"I don't feel enough for Bon-Hwa."

"Feelings can be dangerous."

True, but that was an awful way to live—second-guessing everything, walking through every relationship paranoid.

"Feelings can be wonderful, too." She would much rather focus on that. "I know what it feels like to be loved by you. I know what it feels like to love you, too. That has to give me an advantage."

Of course it did. She knew love. Healthy love. The kind that made your heart feel too big for its chest. The kind that made you thank God before you closed your eyes each night. The kind that made you jump out of bed each morning. Cool, calm, confident, compromising love. And if Rome didn't know what that felt like, she would teach him.

She squeezed her mother's hand. "I got this."

Now all she had to do was go out and get the rest.

•••

"I'm sorry," Rome said.

Amelia laughed. She pushed back in her desk chair and linked her hands behind her head, bending her arms out to the side like a couple of bat wings. "Say it again."

"Don't push your luck." But on second thought, she probably deserved it for the abrupt way he'd left. "I'm sorry," he said again.

"Are you really sorry, or are you only sorry Barry couldn't get you out of your contract?"

"Probably a little of both."

"I'll give you points for honesty." She folded her hands in front of her and studied him with evil green eyes. "Anything else you want to be honest about?"

He shrugged. "Any chance I can have my old job back?"

"Don't push your luck," she said, but something in her almost smile told him there was a chance, and that was excellent.

He needed her on his side now more than ever.

"My turn," she said. "I'm sorry, too."

He did not expect to hear those words. "For what?" he asked skeptically.

"Rome, I pushed you way too far. I thought that dangling the job over your head was the way to get you to listen to and respect me, and it was the wrong approach. It made me no better than you ... or at least the you that used to get all the airtime. I promise to not be a tyrant, if ..." she grinned, "I decide to hire you back."

He smiled, too. It was a strange conversation. Strange company. He wished Jade were here to witness him and Amelia actually getting along.

He glanced at the marketing poster for *JADED ... with Rome Rizzelli* hanging on the wall behind Amelia's desk. "I'm not sure she wants me back."

"Who?" Amelia looked behind her. "Ah. Well, *she* doesn't have a say in it. I'm the station owner." She seemed to rethink those heavy-handed words. "Let me rephrase that. If Jade were an integral part of this station, then she would have a say, but she's not. Not anymore."

The news rocked him. "Did you fire her?"

"Nope. She quit."

"Your little minion finally rebelled."

"She was never my minion, Rome. We weren't plotting against you, and there was no uprising that led to her leaving. She simply wasn't cut out for the job. I guess that's what I get for pushing people too far and expecting too much." She looked thoughtful for a moment, and then the fire was in her eyes again. "But hey, you're back. So silver fucking lining, right?" She slapped her hands on her desk and stood. "I want you on air Monday morning. Jade will just have to deal with it. I'll have your new cohost hired by the end of the month. Now, *she* very well might be my little minion." Amelia left the room on a hearty cackle.

Things were better now, weren't they? He'd apologized. She'd apologized. But still, he wasn't sure. Probably because Amelia was never going to be a pushover. And that was okay. He had every intention of pushing her a little less. Except when it came to one thing:

She didn't have to worry about hiring his new cohost. He was going to convince the old one that right beside him was where she belonged.

Chapter Nineteen

A few hours after unloading on Umma and Halmoni, Jade walked into Ballers' with her shoulders square and her chin up, like it was any other sports bar and just another remote broadcast. She ignored the turnoff to the restrooms and the staircase where she'd first encountered Rome. She didn't entertain a single memory of that kiss or what it had started. At least, she tried not to. She had more important things to think about, like what she was going to say to Amelia to get her job back.

"Hey!" Amelia walked toward her with a headset in one hand and a laptop tucked beneath the other arm. "I have a guest host coming in tonight."

"Oh." Just the way Amelia had said it made Jade think the guest host was a potential replacement. She should've talked to Amelia even before she'd talked to her mother and grandmother. It was kind of crappy to spring this on Amelia now when she may or may not have already lined up someone to take Jade's place. And what if Jade announced she wanted to rescind her resignation only to have Amelia say, "Too late"? How would Jade get through the show after that?

Crap. She was trying to talk herself out of this, wasn't she? Nope. Old habits might die hard, but they did die.

"I declined the teaching position," Jade said.

Amelia's eyes widened. "Interesting."

"I'd like to stay at the station if there's still a place for me."

Amelia unleashed a goofy grin that had Jade feeling off balance. "Oh, there's a place for you."

Thank God. But something in Amelia's expression was still unsettling. Maybe the replacement would take over drive time. Maybe Jade would be forced into another time slot. Which was fine. Wherever Amelia put her, Jade's ratings would be great.

"Where might that place be?" she asked, succumbing to the gnawing curiosity.

Amelia laughed. "We'll talk about it later." And then, she just walked away.

Not exactly what Jade expected from the conversation, but hey, it went well. It did go well, didn't it? There was a place for her at the station.

"If we heckle you during the show, will we get thrown out?"

Jade spun around to see Jillian, Tanya, and MJ smiling at her.

"I was just thinking a few spitballs," Jillian said.

"Keepin' it classy," Tanya said.

Jade chuckled. "Thanks for coming, guys."

"Of course!" MJ pulled her into a hug. "Did you talk to your boss?"

"Just did." They were all looking at her expectantly. "She said we would talk more later, but it sounds like I can stay on at the station."

A series of whoops and cheers followed by some high-fives bolstered Jade. She really was making the right decision—the decision that made *her* happy.

"What about Rome?" Jillian asked.

Good question. "I haven't texted him yet."

Tanya frowned. "Why not?"

"Honestly, I've had a lot on my mind." Not that he wasn't one of those things. "I'm just trying to do this one at a time. I talked to my mother and grandmother. I talked to Amelia. Next, I'll talk to Rome."

MJ studied her. "Did you save him for last because that's the thing you want the most?"

"No." She just assumed she was doing it in order of importance. Which sounded awful now that she thought about it. Maybe she should've called him first.

"Do yourself a favor and text him right now," Jillian said. "While we're all here for moral support and before you chicken out."

"Okay." Jade took a deep breath, knowing once she set this in motion, she couldn't take it back. She typed a simple message:

Hi. I've been thinking about you. Can we talk?

"Good girl," Tanya said.

"And don't be wigged out if he doesn't text back right away." MJ grinned. "Guys play hard to get, too."

"Is that what Tag did?" Jade asked.

"Nah. He was just an emotional wreck."

She almost didn't hear the ding of an incoming text message over their laughter, but then Jillian reached for the phone. "Is that ...?"

"Rome." Jade turned her back on her friends for some semblance for privacy.

I've been thinking about you, too. A talk sounds good.

She almost kissed the screen before she texted back:

Name the time and place.

"Jade?"

She looked up and into the one face she never expected to see here tonight. "Umma?" Make that two faces. "Halmoni? What are you doing here? *In a bar?*"

Her friends folded into the background until she was standing with her mother and grandmother, who looked incredibly out of place in a sports bar filled with twenty- and thirtysomethings.

"We wanted to see you work," Umma said. "We wanted to show you that we support your new career."

"Thank you!" She wrapped them in a hug.

"We can get ice cream afterward," Halmoni said.

Jade grinned. Tradition or not, she had a feeling Halmoni wanted the ice cream more than she wanted Jade to have it. Which was absolutely, positively fine with her. How blessed was she to have these two strong women in her life, watching out for her? Scratch that. She had more than two strong women in her life.

She led Umma and Halmoni over to the table where her friends were now sitting. "Take good care of them," she said to Tanya, and then she pointed at Jillian. "Halmoni, don't let this one have any straws or napkins. She's trouble."

Over the laughter, she heard Amelia's voice. "Chatty Cathy, let's go! You have a show to do."

Yes, she did. And she had a feeling it was going to be epic.

She waved to the table where everyone she loved sat. Well, not quite everyone. One glance at her phone and she saw he hadn't texted back yet, but she was not going to let that bother her.

Maybe he really was playing hard to get.

• • •

"You know you really should play hard to get," Amelia said as she accepted two glasses of beer from the bartender. "It makes for more sexual tension."

Rome rolled his eyes beneath the low brim of his baseball cap and sank further down into the shadows around the bar. "Forgive me if I don't take any more relationship advice from you." Last time was bad enough.

Amelia laughed. "I suppose that's fair. Just make sure you're done with whatever you have to say to her and are ready to go on in about ..." she glanced at her watch, "ten minutes."

"I'll be ready."

She leaned in and spoke directly into his ear. "You two are going to get me huge ratings."

He didn't care about ratings. He only wanted to get the girl.

"Do you want something other than water?" the bartender asked.

Rome shook his head and abandoned the stool. "Not tonight." He needed to be thinking clearly so he could pick the right words.

His phone vibrated as he slid off the barstool and took a step. It was a text message from Tess:

When will you be on?

It was cute how excited she was to have him back on the air, cohosting with Jade. He looked at the clock on his phone and then typed:

About ten minutes. Wish me luck.

At least a dozen "good lucks" followed. His phone was still vibrating with Tess's overzealous well wishes as he made his way through the crowd and closer to the table where Jade was broadcasting.

He could hear her talking about Boltz training camp.

"I don't know why there's any question here," she said. "Minimal full-scale contact at camp has been law for years now. Do you really want to look at all the information we have detailing head trauma and couple that with some of the more high-profile camp injuries and then hit rewind? When you pay someone two million dollars to play, you're paying them to actually play. Why would you want to sabotage yourself?"

He smiled. Here was the part where he would play devil's advocate and tell her that some people might say she was letting a checkbook degrade a sport she supposedly loves. Those same people might even suggest she and anyone who agreed with her could sing "Kumbaya" and then go play flag football, leaving the real game to real men who could handle it. But *he* would never say something like that, never again.

"Okay then."

Her tone of voice made him stop on the outskirts of the crowd pushed into the front of the bar to watch the broadcast.

"Apparently, I have a guest coming on," she said.

That was him. His smile faded on a rush of nerves.

"So we're going to take another quick break, and I'll be back."

He looked at Amelia, who was covertly motioning for him to hurry up and approach the table, where Jade seemed preoccupied with something on her laptop.

She'd been thinking about him. She wanted to talk. She'd asked him to name the time and place. *How 'bout now?* he thought as he pushed through the crowd, feeling jittery. After everything he'd put her through, she still had every right to turn him away.

Jade didn't look up until he was almost on top of the table. Her wide eyes sparkled with surprise, even as her forehead wrinkled with confusion.

"I don't think you presented both sides of the training camp issue," he said slyly.

She smiled briefly. "It's not my job to present both sides. In fact, I was taught to pick a side and go with it. That gets the listeners worked up."

"Whoever taught you that is brilliant."

She made a face. "He likes to think so."

"And what do you think?"

"About what?"

"About me? About us?"

She made a face again and glanced in the direction of Amelia. "This is probably not the best place for this conversation."

"I know, but it can't wait. I mean technically it can, but I've waited too long already to say what needs to be said."

That got her attention. She looked him over thoughtfully. "What needs to be said?"

"Well, for one, I think we can make this work. Us work," he clarified.

She nodded, the faintest hint of a smile on her face. "And what makes you think it will work now when you said it wouldn't work before?"

He gave her a sheepish look. "Some things have changed. *I've* changed. I'm tired of being a stagnant and *jaded* Rome Rizzelli. There's more to life. You know?"

She grinned. "Very clever."

"Thank you. But it's more than that. Really. I've worked some things out with my family," he added, feeling almost desperate to make her understand how serious he was about this. "I'm telling you, it can work ... if you want it to."

She looked around the busy bar, and the longer she went without responding, the more he squirmed. He would do just about anything to get her to try.

"That sounds good to me," she finally said.

He grinned, so big and bold, thankful for the second change. And then, with the help of a whoosh of adrenaline, he was off the mental script he'd made. "You know how I know without a doubt it will work?" He reached for her hand. "Because I love you. It's true. I. Love. You."

She gasped, and for a second there, he thought he'd blown it. Too much too fast.

"You don't have to say it back right now," he said, giving her an out. "I'm prepared to work for it. To earn it."

"Shoot." She pointed to her headset. "Amelia just said my guest host is here. I'm so, so sorry to cut you off like that. Can we finish this discussion later?"

That's when he remembered she'd been wearing the headphones all along and was probably holding her tongue for fear of being overheard.

"Absolutely," he said as he walked around the table. Now that he would be spending five days a week with her and two remote broadcasts a month, they had plenty of time to work out the details.

"What are you doing?" she asked.

"Who, me?" He unleashed a devilish grin. "I'm your guest host."

Jade looked at Amelia, who simply smiled.

"Actually, that's not entirely true. Amelia and I have called a truce. So I'm back ... full time ... with you ... come Monday. How's that sound?" He reached for the headphones, but before he could slide them all the way onto both ears, she grabbed his hand and looked him earnestly in the eyes.

"That sounds wonderful, but ... not as wonderful as this." She grabbed her mic in her hand, effectively muting it, and leaned in. "I love you, too," she whispered. "And from here on out, we're both going to work for it."

"All right, love birds! Two-minute warning." Amelia's voice filled his headphones. "Which is just enough time for me to tell you you're both going to be covering Boltz training camp. I have this idea for a Man vs. Woman that's going to be ratings gold. Who can throw the best block—live from camp. Maybe we can get some Boltz players involved. And Clash players, too. Oh my God! That's brilliant! I amaze myself."

From the looks of Jade's smile, he could tell she thought Amelia was as crazy as he did. But it was definitely crazy in a good way. Otherwise, he wouldn't be here with another shot at everything he could've only dreamed of.

There was no doubt about it. Jade was going to kick his ass when it came to blocking. He could see the tally sheet now. But he didn't care who was keeping score anymore.

Sometimes she would win, and sometimes he would win. *That* was the truth, the only truth he cared about.

And anyone who didn't like it could Rome their ass on out of here.

Acknowledgments

Whenever I wrap up a series, it's bittersweet. After spending so much time with these characters, it's hard to imagine them not rolling around in my head. But I'm thrilled to know they will live on with each new reader. Thank you to everyone who gave this team of women football players a chance. I know it was a stretch for some of you. After all, these are definitely not your mother's romance heroines.

I couldn't have delved into this world without the help of certain people. My husband, who spent time as a team physician for a Pittsburgh female full tackle football team. My editor, who saw promise in this idea in the first place. And for this book especially, Adam Crowley, senior producer and host for Steelers Nation Radio, who answered my e-mails and texts almost instantly—even when he was in the throes of training camp. Thank you. Thank you. Thank you.

I'm so blessed to be able to tell these stories. I'm even more blessed to have people like you to read them.

About the Author

Elley Arden is a born and bred Pennsylvanian who has lived as far west as Utah and as far north as Wisconsin. She drinks wine like it's water (a slight exaggeration), prefers a night at the ballpark to a night on the town, and believes almond English toffee is the key to happiness. Elley writes books with charming characters, emotional stories, and sexy romance. For a complete list of Elley's books, visit *www.elleyarden.com*.

More from This Crimson Author
Crossing Lines Elley Arden

Jillian Bell flipped down the visor on her rusted Volvo wagon and assessed the damage on her face. Dark circles or caked mascara from the night before, bloodshot eyes, and hair like something from a static-cling science experiment. *Yikes.* She was a complete mess. Thankfully, it was all fixable.

She reached into the glove box that doubled as her "band promoter Rx kit." No party-girl-by-night and football-player-by-day could live without eye drops, baby wipes, hair ties, and chewing gum. Under a mess of fast-food napkins, crinkled promo flyers, Advil, condoms, guitar picks, hard candy, and cigarette lighters, she found the essentials that would deem her passable enough to keep Coach Howl off her ass.

One energy drink and three sticks of spicy cinnamon gum later, Jillian climbed out of her car and headed for the locker room. *No harm, no foul.*

"Oh my God!" Jade Wren, Jillian's new roommate and the Clash's starting center, pounced the minute Jillian walked into the locker room. "Where the heck have you been for the past two days? I thought something bad happened to you!"

"I was out having fun, and fun is never bad," Jillian said with a smile.

"It is when it makes you late." Tanya Martin, offensive linewoman and Jillian's ex-roommate, made a face and then pushed past Jillian and out the door.

Did she say late? Jillian looked at her phone. "What are you talking about? It's only 5:37. Practice doesn't start until 6:00."

MJ Rooney, the quarterback, shook her head. "Wrong. Coach e-mailed on Saturday night to say we're starting fifteen minutes early today." MJ followed Tanya out of the locker room.

Well, that sucked. Jillian didn't remember much about Saturday night, and she hadn't checked her e-mails in days. "It's okay." She flashed a cocky grin at Jade. "I still have..." she looked at her phone again, "six minutes. I'll be out there before anybody misses me."

As the locker room emptied out, Jillian flew through her prepractice ritual, skipping the usual taping of her ankles and bopping around to Eminem's "Lose Yourself." Everything was going beautifully, until she reached inside her duffle bag for her cleats. They weren't there.

"Shit!" Where could they be? *The trunk.* She'd tossed them back there after Saturday's game because they were muddy. Without a second thought, she sprinted to her car, and by the time she made it to the field, it was 5:47.

Oh well, at least she hadn't missed much. Her teammates were still huddled around Coach Howl. With any luck, her late arrival wouldn't even be noticed. She sidled up to Tanya and tried to look like she'd always been standing there.

"If anyone can explain to me what went wrong on Saturday, I'd love to hear it," Coach Howl said. But he didn't wait for anyone to speak up. He kept right on railing them over the fifty-four to seven loss.

What a drag. Jillian tried to tune him out. Her eyes skipped to the unfamiliar man standing behind Coach. *Daaaamn.* That man was fine. Fairly young, too. Thick, blond hair. Bold, blue eyes. Rugged face. And biceps that looked like they lifted small cars instead of weights. That was the kind of man that drew you in like a tractor beam and made you lick your lips in case you were drooling.

The gorgeous man took a few fluid steps and stopped beside Coach Howl.

"Who is *that?*" Tanya asked.

"Thor." Jillian said reverently. "And girl, I'd sell my soul to see his hammer."

Tanya chuckled.

Coach raised a hand above his head, signaling for everyone to quiet down. "Coach Malloy is no longer with us."

Wait! What? There were expressions of shock and murmurs all around her, but for once, Jillian was speechless. Coach Malloy was her "dude." He'd said they were kindred spirits, because they worked beautifully together, even sang everything from rock classics to eighties music during team stretches. He didn't rag on her for talking out of turn, showing off in the end zone, or running a little late. He was a blast, and when it came to football, they were on the exact same page. They'd made plans for this season. Big plans. They were going to prove a women's football team could run a wicked West Coast offense. And yeah, so the first three games—all losses—didn't have them off to a roaring start, but they still had time ... or so she'd thought.

"You fired him?!" She lifted her chin when Coach Howl shot her a death stare.

"He resigned," Coach said.

"*Bullshit*," she coughed into her hand. Coach Malloy probably got the blame for the losses. It was no secret that this season, Coach Howl, who doubled as the running backs coach, wanted more emphasis on the running game.

Coach ignored her and moved on. "It's never easy to change coaches in the middle of a season, which means we have a lot of work to do. There will be several adjustments to make. Namely, I'd like to introduce you to your..."

At that exact moment, she remembered Thor. *Oh my God.* It couldn't be.

"... new offensive coordinator..."

It was.

"... and receivers coach ..."

Which meant Thor was "in charge" of her. Hot or not, she wasn't happy.

Jillian glance at her teammates to see how they were taking the news. Shocked faces all around.

"... Carter Howl, my son."

Oh no he didn't. Her head whipped around so fast she felt a sharp pain in her neck. Coach Howl replaced Coach Malloy with his son!

"You've got to be kidding me," she said a little too loudly, then grabbed her sore neck and rubbed. What was that bit about the apple not falling far from the tree? If that was true, then their passing game was doomed.

The younger Coach Howl looked at her, and—*ooh!*—those magic eyes produced a heat that pierced through her to the center of her neck pain, until she couldn't even feel her toes.

I'm cured, she thought, followed by, *maybe he won't be so bad.* In fact, maybe he wasn't anything like his father at all. Maybe he was the black sheep in his family—just like she was.

He looked away, patted his father on the shoulder, and then stepped up to address the team. "Ladies, I'm honored to be here," he said. "Rather than bore you with details about my football background, let me just say that I have plenty of experience with both the sport and the discipline needed to get the job done. Winning isn't rocket science. The team that wins works harder and longer than the losing team, and the team that wins knows how to stay out of trouble—on and off the field."

Why the hell was he looking at her?

She rolled her eyes. He narrowed his.

"*You* were late," he said.

She looked behind her, knowing full well he was talking to her. "Barely late."

At her response, he stood straighter and narrowed his eyes until they were slits. "Late is late, and it's not tolerated on this field." He made a whirling signal with his finger. "Laps ... until I tell you to stop."

He had to be kidding. She was the best player on this team. She'd scored every single one of the twenty-one points they'd scored so far this season.

She crossed her arms and looked at Coach Howl. He was no help. The faintest smile curved his lips.

"I miss Coach Malloy already!" she yelled as she threw her helmet to the sidelines and started jogging around the track.

By the time Thor deigned to release her from lap running, stretching was over and her mood was foul. She got in line and readied to run routes.

"Partying got the best of you this weekend, didn't it?" MJ asked.

"Never." They just had a new OC with a stick up his ass. Or a hammer. She looked at him and snickered.

He paced the sidelines, watching the team's every move, looking way too serious for his own good. *He's going to have a heart attack*, she thought. Which wouldn't be terrible. At least then he couldn't coach anymore.

He stopped pacing and stood with his feet shoulder width apart, a position that showed off strong thigh muscles beneath his thin athletic pants. She bet he had a six-pack. What a shame. God had formed a whole lot of fine man around one big asshole.

"Second group!" Coach yelled. "Slant. I want to see the head tilt."

Jillian stepped up to the line and got into her stance. The instant the whistle blew, everything else faded away.

A couple hours later, she was sweaty and exhausted, and that made everything else tolerable.

"Bell!"

Oh hell. Thor's voice boomed above the noisy chatter of her teammates, who were stampeding toward the locker room. She pretended like she didn't hear him.

"Bell, I know you can hear me."

What was with this guy? She stopped but didn't give him the satisfaction of turning around.

"You were five minutes late today, so tomorrow you will be fifteen minutes early."

Which didn't make any sense. She spun around. "I already paid my debt by running laps."

"Your debt will be paid when I say it's been paid. Fifteen minutes before everyone else. Right here." He pointed to the field. "Or you'll give me fifteen minutes on the bench this Saturday. Your choice."

What a jerk!

When she reached the locker room, she threw her cleats into her locker with a satisfying bang.

"We're going out tonight," she said to Jade emphatically. She needed shots of Patrón and loud dance music to wash away the suck of dealing with Tweedledee and Tweedledum of the Gridiron. "You and you..." she pointed at Tanya and MJ, "are more than welcome if your balls..." she chuckled, "and chains give you permission." Both of them had moved out of her apartment and in with guys who took up way too much of their time. What a drag! Having to ask permission to go out? No thank you. Jillian hadn't answered to anyone since she'd left home at nineteen. And she liked it that way.

"Going out again isn't going to get the new OC off your back," MJ said.

She did not want to talk about Thor.

"Maybe you should stay in tonight," Jade said. "We could watch a movie."

"That's boring," Jillian said.

Tanya gave her a knowing look. "I think you could use some boring. You were late for practice, Jill. That's a big deal, even for you."

Her frustration peaked. "It was five minutes!" she yelled. "I've been twenty minutes late before and Malloy never batted an eyelash! Man, I can't believe Coach sacked him to give his own son a job. Nepotism is the fucking worst. I bet he's a shitty—"

"Your phone's ringing." Jade cut in on her rant, looking hesitant to even bring it up. She pointed at the white and silver iPhone vibrating on the bench. "See?"

Jillian saw the name Wendy Novick flash on the screen. "It's my sister," she said, and her stomach hollowed out. Two months ago, Wendy had given birth to her first child, a boy, who had been diagnosed with a congenital heart defect. Things weren't exactly good between Jillian and her family. She'd only seen her nephew via Facebook so far, and phone calls were rare. What if it was more bad news about Caleb?

"I should answer this," she said. MJ and Tanya were looking at her with concern.

Jillian wandered off in the direction of the training room where it was quiet. "Hello?"

"Hi. It's me ... Wendy."

"I know who it is, Wen. You're in my contacts. You show up on Caller ID." And even if she didn't, one word spoken in that sweet voice was all Jillian needed to recognize her little sister. "Is everything okay?" The words felt tacky on her tongue.

Wendy hesitated. "We're still waiting on an official date for his heart surgery." A long, heavy silence filled the line, and Jillian dropped into a nearby chair. "You're seeing the pictures I've been posting on Facebook, right?"

An image of her cute nephew popped into her head, and Jillian swallowed past the lump in her throat. "I am. He's a doll baby." He really was beautiful, and her sister looked so happy in all those photos. "I can't believe you're a mom now."

"I can't imagine not being a mom. I can't believe I ever *wasn't* a mom." Her soft chuckle was tinged with sadness.

"When are you supposed to hear about the surgery?"

"I don't know. This week, I hope. But, Jillie, you have to come meet him ... that's why I'm calling." Her sister paused. "I want you to come to his christening."

You could've knocked her over with a feather. "Seriously?"

"Yes, I want you to hold him before..." Wendy's voice cracked. "I don't know how long he will be in the hospital after the surgery, and I don't know how long it will be before people can hold him again. You want to meet him, don't you?"

"Of course I do." But the christening would probably be the social event of the year in Charity. The whole damn town would be there. Her parents, of course. Her jerk off of a brother-in-law, Bob. All those judgmental old church biddies and their redneck husbands. Not to mention the right Reverend G. Keller Winters, Jillian's ex-fiancé. She made a face. "Why don't I just come in for a quiet visit another time?"

"Please." Wendy's voice shook. "We hired a photographer. I'm going to scrapbook the whole thing. I want you to be there. I want Caleb to look back at these books someday and see you were there."

Oh God, her sister was crying. For a fleeting moment, Jillian was thrown back fifteen years to when their father was deployed with the Army, and Wendy cried herself to sleep every night he was gone. Just how risky would this surgery be? Considering how small the kid was, probably pretty damn risky. She should go, for Wendy and the baby, despite everyone else.

But it wasn't that simple.

"I'm in the middle of a rough football season." If Thor got his panties in a bunch over her missing five minutes of practice, what would he do if she missed a game?

"I know, but I was hoping you could work something out. Charity is only two hours from Cleveland. And he's being baptized on a Sunday. Surely you don't play on the Lord's Day. I mean, I would love for you to be here for everything. The layette breakfast is on Saturday morning. But I understand if you can only make it to the church on Sunday and the luncheon afterward. I'll take what I can get." Wendy's exhale echoed on the other end. "I want you there, Jillie. I *need* you there."

Wendy was quite possibly the only person in the world she had trouble saying no to, and under the circumstances, saying no would be a major jerk move. "Okay," she conceded. "I'll figure something out."

"Thank you. Thank you so much!"

Jillian felt a smile stretch across her face.

"Just promise me you'll tone it down," Wendy continued. "No alcohol this time. No cursing. Cover the tattoos. Please."

Jillian's muscles tensed. There was always a catch. But this time, how could she say no? After a long exhale, she said, "I'll give it a shot ... for you."

When the call ended, she wandered into the locker room.

"What's wrong?" Tanya asked immediately.

"Nothing's wrong." She put the phone on the top shelf of her locker and grabbed her towel off the hook.

"Liar. I can tell by your face."

"Nothing's wrong-wrong. Wendy wants me at Caleb's christening."

"That's good! It's an olive branch. Girl, you're an aunt. Embrace that, and kick the rest of the crap aside."

She wished she could, but going back to Charity was like walking through a land mine. She hated it! So much she could count on one hand the number of times she'd been back in the last seven years.

"Are you going to go?" MJ asked. The crinkled look on her face said she knew Jillian would at least try to get out of it.

"I feel like I have to. I mean he's sick. I should've seen him already." God, what kind of aunt did that make her? A shitty one, that was for sure.

"When is it?" Jade asked.

"Two weeks. It's a home game, so I could technically drive to Charity Saturday evening and then come home Sunday night. I wouldn't miss any football that way."

"That sounds great!" Jade smiled. Of course she did. She didn't know the whole story.

"It *would be* great if Bob wasn't there." Jillian exchanged glances with Tanya and MJ, because they knew exactly what she was talking about.

"Who's Bob?" Jade asked.

"Bob is Wendy's husband, and he hates me."

"For good reason," MJ added.

Jillian rolled her eyes. "Maybe."

Tanya laughed. "Definitely."

"Why does he hate you?" Jade was on the edge of the bench.

"I brought alcohol to the wedding, and I shared it with the best man, Bob's brother."

Jade looked confused. "Okay. What's wrong with that? Everybody drinks at weddings."

MJ sat beside Jade. "Charity is a dry town. No booze anywhere. Not even at weddings."

Jade grimaced.

"I know, right?" Jillian asked. "I just wanted to have fun. I mean my ex was the officiant. I had to stand through an entire ceremony listening to him talk about how a woman's place is subservient to her husband, who is her lord on earth." She pawed at her neck. "It made my skin crawl, but I respected Wendy, and I behaved..." she paused at a look from MJ, "until the reception. I couldn't stand another minute of all those self-righteous townies judging me. I had to let off a little steam." And through the years, Bruce had always been willing to let loose with her.

"I'm not sure you *had to* have sex with the best man in a broom closet." Tanya's head bobbed with attitude.

"Bob found them," MJ said, filling in the torrid conclusion for Jade. "He opened the door and got a fine shot of his little brother's ass."

Jade gasped. The other two laughed, having heard the story at least a dozen times.

Jillian smacked a hand to her forehead and rubbed it across her face. "I was drunk."

The icing on the whole bitter cake had been her parents throwing her out of the house the morning after. Going home for the first time since *that* was going to make this trip a million times harder.

"Wait a minute. Did I hear that right? Your ex is a priest?" Jade's eyes widened.

"A preacher," Jillian corrected. "But he wasn't a preacher when I was with him, and I wasn't..." she lifted a strand of electric blue hair, "like this. I was nineteen. It was a long time ago." Almost ten years. But she still didn't like seeing him, and she hated the judgment and pity in his eyes. She hated even more the town's collective opinion that she'd gone to hell after she'd turned down the love of a good man. Criticism like that made her do stupid things to prove that she was just fine the way she was.

"That's why Wendy wants me to clean up my act." Jillian cringed. "She said no drinking, no cursing, and cover up the tattoos." She looked down at the colorful collage climbing her right arm from wrist to elbow. "If it were anyone else asking me to do that, I'd tell them to go fuck themselves."

"Wait." Tanya gaped at her. "You mean to tell me you're going to do it? You're going to get rid of the blue streaks in your hair, wear long sleeves, and watch your mouth all weekend?"

"It's not *all* weekend. I'll be there less than forty-eight hours." Jillian ignored the tension in her chest. "I can manage it."

"I don't know why you would," MJ said. "It's not okay for them to ask you to be someone else simply to be good enough to meet your nephew."

Jillian sighed. "It's not like that ... at least, not for Wendy. She's fine with the way I am. She's just trying to protect me from the people who aren't."

MJ shook her head in disagreement. "I still don't like it."

"I still don't think you're capable of doing it," Tanya said.

Jillian glared at Jade. "You want to weigh in with some negativity, too? Make it unanimous?"

"Well..." Jade bit into her bottom lip. "It seems very stressful. I'm afraid you'll crack without serious support. Maybe one of us should go with you."

Ooh! She resented their lack of confidence. "I'll be fine," she said. In fact, better than fine. She would prove to them that she could be boring for one freaking weekend.

How hard could it be?

Praise for *Crossing Lines*:

"I devoured the story ... Fun, sexy, and filled with smart ass side comments (and humor), this book is a great way to enter the world of the Cleveland Clash series." —4 stars, Art Books Coffee

"Arden never fails to create wonderful tales that capture your heart and your imagination. This novel is no exception. It was a fantastic, heartfelt novel that held me throughout."—5 stars, Pure Jonel

For more from Elley Arden, check out:

Running Interference

Praise for *Running Interference*:

"Readers need not be sports fans to appreciate the strong female lead Arden has created in Tanya. Adding to the entertainment is the sweat-inducing physicality that occurs both on the field and off." – *Library Journal*

"Arden creates a heroine worthy of the MVP title ... this sports romance [is] one to root for!" — Heroes and Heartbreakers

"I love the focus on women in sports, a very underappreciated and underexposed focal point for novels. The contrast between men's and women's pro football was quite poignant. Arden, writing with her usual well-polished, light-hearted style combines this all into an unforgettable package." — Pure Jonel

"I'm a sucker for second chance romances and *Running Interference* did not disappoint. This is my first Elley Arden read and I can guarantee it won't be my last. She has a unique writing style. Simple, yet strong with fluid and easy dialogue, you can't help but dive in and not come up until you're finished." — Eat Sleep Read Reviews

The Kemmons Brothers Baseball Series

Save My Soul

Change My Mind

Heal My Heart

Take Me Out

Praise for the Kemmons Brothers series:

"Nel and Gray have a lot of fun and challenging things to face . . . You will fall in love with them both . . . For a fun, sweet and very entertaining read, don't miss *Change My Mind* by Elley Arden." —Harlequin Junkie

"...Elley Arden really manages to evoke a barrage of emotions in her readers. She really has a way of creating novels that will touch you." —Texas Book Nook

"This is one of those novels that combines a multiplicity of different elements, backgrounds, and social stigmas into a single whole that will take your breath away and leave you reeling. Arden's brilliant descriptions will paint a picture you won't soon forget." —Pure Jonel

Harmony Falls Novels

Crashing the Congressman's Wedding

Battling the Best Man

Marrying the Wrong Man

Praise for the Harmony Falls series:

"The ending was my all-time favorite . . . This is definitely an AMAZING book that I recommend to all!" —Mamival's Books

"Good things come when you least expect it—at least I did with this book. I didn't expect to laugh, cry, and fall in love. But Elley Arden did those things to me, and after that short read, I think I'm coming back for more from this author." —Book Freak

Emerald Springs Legacy

Trouble Brewing

Chad's Chance